The LOST LINER

by Robert Cromie

With a new introduction by Diarmuid Kennedy

avalard™
GORTAHERON BOOKS

A Gortaheron Book

Published by Avalard Publishing
Annadorn, Co. Down, UK
March 2012

www.avalardpublishing.com

ISBN: 978-1-908566-20-1 (Paperback)
ISBN: 978-1-908566-21-8 (Ebook)

The Lost Liner text © Avalard Publishing 2012
Introduction © Diarmuid Kennedy 2012

avalard™

Gortaheron is a trademark of Avalard Publishing.

All Rights Reserved.
This publication may not be reproduced, recorded, stored or transmitted by any means in existence now or yet to be invented, without prior written permission of the publishers.
We hope you enjoy this book.

CONTENTS

	INTRODUCTION	5
I	A Fall In The Barometer.	17
II	The Cradle Of The Deep.	33
III	Clear Away The Boats.	46
IV	Alone!	57
V	In The Depths Of The Sea.	66
VI	Duty.	77
VII	Margery Improves.	88
VIII	The Uncharted Island.	98
IX	Confined To Barracks.	111
X	The Harbour Bar Was Moaning.	128
XI	A Night Of Terror.	139
XII	The Flowing Tide Comes In.	150
XIII	A Forlorn Hope.	165
XIV	Derelict.	178
XV	Good-Bye, Margery Bute.	194
XVI	"No Cards".	205
	PUBLISHER'S ACKNOWLEDGEMENTS AND A NOTE ON THIS EDITION	215

INTRODUCTION

A note on *The Lost Liner*

ROBERT CROMIE'S *The Lost Liner* is certainly an extraordinary curiosity. Published in 1898, and originally entitled *The Unchartered Island*, it tells of George Drury and Margery Bute, passengers on board the liner *Maori*. While en route from San Francisco to Auckland drama unfolds when the vessel is caught in a typhoon. The novel is however a much stranger brew than a simple tale of adventure on the high seas.

Among the most striking elements in *The Lost Liner* are the parallels with the fate that befell the *Titanic* over a decade after this novel was published. The *Maori* is described as "unsinkable" and when the call is made to abandon ship, a man attempting to rush the lifeboat is shot by the captain. Famously the *Titanic* was also considered "practically unsinkable" and at least one crew member fired a pistol to control panicking passengers.

That Cromie, who lived in Belfast, should write about a liner is not surprising. In the five years prior to the novel's publication the Belfast-based shipbuilders

Harland and Wolff (who later would build the *Titanic*) produced over 354,000 tonnes of shipping. A fascination with marine design can be found in his other novels, and apart from fiction he wrote about marine steam turbines and the construction of ocean liners.

Cromie's hero George Drury sees the liner as a symbol of man's progress. Even as he sits on the deck of the crippled *Maori* he says without irony that he considers "a first-class ocean steamship a grander wonder of the world than the biggest pyramid in Egypt: the one is only a monument to brute force and slavery, the other is a triumph of brains and free labour." His words echo the opinions of the author who wrote in 1904: "However we look back into the vistas of the past we see man as a mechanic, and we find that in proportion to his proficiency in mechanics was his advance in civilisation."

Despite both the author's and hero's admiration of the liner as a symbol of human achievement, it flounders. The *Maori* fails, because it represents a microcosm of limiting social structures - in common with the real ocean liners of the day. The confined and demarcated areas on board serve to underline distinctions based on wealth and class. Prior to the typhoon the relationship between Margery and George is impossible because Margery is a "saloon passenger" and George "second-class." The old order represented by their fellow travellers must be swept away so that Cromie can explore other ideas.

When cast up on the Unchartered Island, and apparently free from the strictures of society, Margery and George are however still symbolically captive. This is partly because they cling to the rules of the world they have temporarily left, but also because they are restrained and frightened by the power of nature itself. Like Prospero's island this is a place of both magic and terror. Initially it is fantastical with "gaudy-plumaged birds", "multi-coloured fish" and a tide that flows "in a phosphorescent cascade." But this paradise seems to frighten. The movement of the sea at night apparently scares Margery with its suggestive motion: "the great pulse of the Pacific moved the still water of the lagoon, and caused its placid bosom to swell in a long, slow answering heave, over which the "Star of Asia" rose easily, and then fell gently down...This arrested Margery's wandering fancy. The recall was something of a shock."

During this dreamy boat trip Margery sings a number of popular ballads, finishing with "Rocked in the Cradle of the Deep". While her other songs are romantic, this is religious in tone with lyrics by Emma Hart Willard (1787-

1870), a pioneer in women's education in the USA who opened that country's first academic school for women. Thus Cromie subtly manages to introduce themes of women's equality and belief as sub-texts even at the novel's apparently most traditional scene.

This lush picture is soon forgotten as the place takes on an altogether more sinister atmosphere when the sea deposits a dreadful cargo on the beach. From this point the island is a nightmarish and violent place, the sea a "seething mass" and the beach emitting a "harsh growl" as the pebbles are ground by the tide.

George's sexual attraction to Margery is quite starkly implied by Cromie. A man and woman castaway alone on an island carries obvious implications and Cromie was clearly not above exploiting the reader's expectations. One of the most arresting scenes is when George, convinced that he and Margery are facing a slow and certain death, decides to kill her in order to save her prolonged suffering. It is not difficult to imagine what Cromie is hinting at here: "He put his hand on the girl's neck and found that her tightly buttoned dress covered her throat where he intended to strike. It resisted his fingers. He had neither time nor patience to unfasten it. So he slipped the point of the knife below it, and with a long tearing "zip" the cloth gave way before the keen edge...the knife is a brutal weapon. And it was such a soft and slender throat! He might yet have paused, only that nothing now appealed to him, save the craving to get the thing over and be done with it."

The novel is not without humour, Cromie's depiction of the German, French and American passengers is stereotyping of a hilarious order, and the stiff upper-lipped crew are also straight from central casting. The Captain comments that he shot a passenger trying to jump the lifeboat queue to "let the others know that this is a British ship!"

One other more oblique instance of humour can be found in the strange editorial intervention on page 79. The reference here to the philosopher Adam Smith sees Cromie poking elaborate fun at George Drury's intellectual pretentions. Similarly the shooting of an Albatross by the passenger, also called Smith, who is a member of the "thirteen club" signposts the approaching disaster in neon.

As unhappy in their tropical Eden as they were on the *Maori*, George and Margery are actually (and metaphorically) lost in an unchartered region. George, for all his radical ideas, ultimately conforms; the opportunity for liberation offered to the couple on the island is not grasped and instead they cling to convention. Back in civilisation the couple are misfits living uneasily with the conventions of society. George is again the unhappy man the reader met at the beginning. Margery is now alone and compromised by the public scandal surrounding her time on the island with George.

The novel's abrupt ending reflects the predicament of its central characters and the problematic issues their story raises. Margery and George are united "off stage", leaving the reader with plenty to contemplate.

A note on Robert Cromie

ROBERT CROMIE was born in 1856 in Clough, County Down, in what is now Northern Ireland. He was educated at the Royal Belfast Academical Institute and worked until around 1900 for the Ulster Bank. Between 1888 and 1904 he published nine novels and two collections of short stories.

Cromie's second novel *A Plunge into Space* was published in 1890 and largely established his reputation. It describes a trip to Mars made by a strange collection of men including a scientist, an artist, a journalist and an Irish politician. On Mars they find a highly advanced, if somewhat unexciting, civilization. While the trip ends in tragedy, the novel is not without humour. A Martian comments to the Irishman that his county must be very large and cover at least half of the Earth. Having asked the alien how she reached that conclusion the answer is that "it occupied more of the newspaper than all the other nations of the earth put together".

When over a decade later H.G. Wells' *The First Men in the Moon* was published it contained some striking similarities. Such was the closeness that Cromie wrote two letters to *The Academy* journal. In the first he apologizes for having "subconsciously plagiarised beforehand" Wells' work and in the next he spells out eight elements which both books have in common. Certainly it is difficult to read the novels without feeling that Wells had at least borrowed heavily. Both open with the discovery of a material that is immune to Earth's gravity and a very similar globe-shaped spacecraft appears in both books.

A Plunge into Space was popular, remaining in print for some 20 years. One edition is dedicated to the French writer Jules Verne and contains an introduction attributed to Verne, praising the skill of his pupil. However a scholar writing in *Science Fiction Studies* has questioned the authenticity of Verne's connection with Cromie. He points out that no French translation of the book existed at the time and that Verne's English was not good enough for him to have read the novel. It is also curious that if the introduction *was* written by Verne, it makes it the only one he ever wrote. The explanation offered is either the introduction was concocted by Cromie and his publishers, or that it was in fact written by Verne's son Michael. Further evidence for questioning Verne's introduction is the fact that elsewhere he found

Wells' anti-gravity concept laughable, so why does he apparently praise it in one novel and deride it in another?

Cromie's next novel *The Crack of Doom* was published in 1895. It is the story of a scientist bent on destroying the world because he finds it without any purpose or plan. Brande, the scientist, sees nature as "founded upon and begotten of a system of everlasting suffering as hideous as the fantastic nightmares of religious maniacs", with "wholesale murder" as its "first law". His method of destruction is to be the atomic bomb. He demonstrates that the "atom is destructible" by disintegrating a drop of water with catastrophic results, "the sea behind us burst into flame, followed by the sound of an explosion so frightful that we were almost stunned by it." Cromie is thus the first writer to depict an atomic explosion, it was almost twenty years before H.G. Wells' description of one in *The World Set Free*.

Cromie's apparently mad or evil scientist is a rather more complex character. Brande is not motivated by financial gain, pure madness or anger, but instead by a scientific understanding of the universe which leads him to the logical conclusion that it must be destroyed. We find something similar in Cromie's 1902 novel *The New Messiah* where the global financial system is threatened by organised assassinations and plots to destabilise the markets. Zietsman, the central conspirator, speaks of dispensing with the "swashbuckler" millionaires and nations who ride "rough shod over the world". In both novels Cromie is painting a world where religion seems to be either replaced by science, or unable to answer the questions it raises. The ideas raised in *The Crack of Doom* prompted William Gladstone to write to Cromie expressing his opinion that while he was "grateful to Science for all it has done, and is doing...Christianity stands in no need of it."

Cromie was a keen golfer and the captain of Ormeau Golf Club in 1898. In his last novel *El Dorado* a character says that there is "something strangely exhilarating in the flight of a ball. It is a joy that was strong when the world was young, and it seems to have grown no older with our trips around the sun. It may be an inheritance...from our Mother Earth herself, which is only a big ball spinning in space." For those not gripped by golf it does often seem like a glimpse of eternity, but Cromie's words cast it an entirely different light. It is possible to imagine Robert Cromie in the landscaped world of the Ormeau Park with the gantries of the shipyards visible to the south dreaming of interplanetary travel and global destruction as a small white ball arcs above the trees.

Cromie's output was not greeted with universal praise, *The Saturday Review* wrote of *El Dorado*: "That Mr. Cromie knows very little about archaeology is of less importance than the fact that he cannot construct a really readable sensational story."

Robert Cromie died at the age of 51 in his rooms at 95 South Parade, just yards from his beloved Ormeau Golf Club, on April 7th 1907.

Diarmuid Kennedy
Belfast, February 2012

(Elements of this Introduction were previously published in *Verbal Magazine*, issue 33, October 2010)

Chapter I.
A FALL IN THE BAROMETER.

"ANYMORE for the shore? More for the shore?"

The quartermasters were shouting it on deck. Below, the stewards called it from cabin to cabin. The last bell had sounded and the five minutes of grace were nearly up. Reluctant friends were parted and the stay-at-homes cleared out with despatch. The captain and his pilot were in their places on the bridge. The third officer had his hand on the telegraph:

"Gangways ashore!"

Handkerchiefs began to wave as these crashed heavily upon the dock.

"Seems like the sound of the clods upon a coffin lid," a thin, shabbily-dressed little woman said to her neighbour, with a dry sob and a somewhat gruesome association of ideas. She was seeing her son off and never expected to see him again.

"Bear up. It'll be over in a minute," the other woman answered in a kind voice, although a complete stranger to the first.

"Let go all! Slow astern!"

The Oceana Shipping Company's *S.S. Maori* backed out slowly amid a chorus of farewells.

"I'll write from Honolulu!"

"And you'll write every mail?"

"Good-bye again!"

"God bless you, my boy!"

As the *Maori* backed out, a fashionably dressed girl stood on the fore end of the lower bridge and watched the people on shore. A young fellow standing beside her was also looking idly toward the wharf. He was pushed by an excited passenger and so jostled her slightly. Raising his cap he muttered a word of regret, without turning to see whom he had knocked against. The girl accepted the apology with a good-humoured nod, and did not look round either. Had these two known what a few days would bring forth, they would surely have been more interested in each other than in a crowd of strangers, amongst whom they did not recognise a single face.

The slow smashing strokes of the propeller quickened slightly. A cheer, with a sob or two in it, was raised on shore. The passengers cheered back. Assisted by a tug-boat, the *Maori* straightened up and went slowly down the bay and out through the Golden Gate. Then the pilot was taken off, the course set, the engines put to full speed, and before long one of the numerous "finest harbours in the world" was on the far horizon.

"That was Cliff House on the South Head," a big, blonde German said, in good English, by way of starting the conversation in the second-class smoking room.

"Giddy place, Cliff House!" a youngster with a cigarette put in. He spoke with the complete knowledge of one who had been half-an-hour in it "Don`t you think so?" he asked a young, thoughtful looking Englishman named Drury—George Drury.

"I really don't know anything about it," Drury answered, carelessly. "I only arrived in San Francisco yesterday, so I had not much time to go about." He seemed anxious to be left to himself. It was done without demur.

A Californian here joined this group, and while they are making the acquaintance of each other I seize the convenient opportunity to acquaint the reader with some necessary information regarding, one of them, and another who was a first-class passenger. Before dealing with them, however, it must be explained that the incidents in the early stages of the voyage of the *Maori* do not closely concern this story. They will, therefore, be hastily passed over; indicated rather than described.

Those characters, too, who disappear early in the narrative need not detain us more than a moment. The central figures, however, require a little more elaboration.

These central characters are only two: a man and a woman. The man, George Drury, was the second-cabin passenger of the *Maori*, from San Francisco for Auckland. He was a tall, slender, but wiry specimen of the British youth; little more than a lad in years, but with large ideas—mainly, it must be admitted, about himself. Full of physical courage, and with more muscle than you would suppose at a first glance, he was wanting in one important element in the achievement of complete success. He was self-conscious, sensitive, perhaps a little sentimental. Anyhow, he could not stand being snubbed, no matter what or how great the favour might be for which this price must be paid. Besides, he was without that steadiness of purpose which is necessary to achieve any measure of success—or he was too easily interested in novel ideas and methods, which produces the same want of result. In short, he was too academic, although he had not had the disadvantage of a university education. This was fatal.

Drury had tried art, and found that, so far as he was concerned, it promised to be very "long," indeed:

business, and discovered that it was incompatible; and, finally, he had tried literature, without result. To literature, for which he had really that instinctive bias out of which may ultimately be hammered a very creditable success, he had given what he considered a fair trial—a six month`s trial. Notwithstanding that many very tolerable authors have taken more time than that to arrive at their position, Drury was satisfied that he had failed. He was in too great a hurry to be famous, and so could not afford the time to fulfil the terms of the usual indenture. Having failed at home, he was going abroad, where it was probable his latter end would be worse than his first. He himself, indeed, was not very hopeful. In evidence of this, he was growing an embryonic beard, which spoilt his rather handsome face. He did this just to show that he was growing careless of the conventionalities of civilization. It is a bad sign in a young man.

Miss Margery Bute, a saloon passenger, was the woman referred to. It was she who had stood on the lower bridge as the *Maori* backed out from the dock at San Francisco, and it was Drury who had apologised to her so carelessly for his unintentional rudeness. Her father was going out to a Colonial Governorship, in which it was hoped by his political enemies that he would make as much of a mess as it was possible to expect from a simple-minded and not particularly gifted man. He was travelling to his colony by a roundabout route; but he was in no hurry, and he was anxious, when on the journey, to "do" the States—in the physical, not financial, sense of the slang, of course. Miss Margery was going with her father to manage the Government household, although very young for that exacting office. She was very well dressed, and was very good-looking. She had fine blue eyes, well-marked brows, thin straight nose, and possessed a treasure beyond price in her hair. This hair had once been tersely described by the belle of a county ball—"red." But that was after Captain Mortimer had sat out three dances with Miss Bute, forgetting that for one of these his name was on the county belle's card. Captain Mortimer had ten thousand a year. Margery's hair may pass.

Margery looked well in anything she wore, and her figure did her tailor credit rather than *vice-versa*. To judge from the number of men who were always hanging about her she could make herself very agreeable when she chose. And she generally did choose when the men were about. She was thus the most important personality on the *Maori* next to the Captain. That she was partly aware of this might be assumed from her authoritative manner on deck, and concluded from the conversation of her maid.

Miss Bute noticed the second-cabin passenger leaning over the rail on the second morning out. His handsome face, and graceful, if slightly woebegone attitude (he was really very homesick), appealed to her sympathy. She spared him an infinitesimal glance of half contemptuous pity, and felt "good" for the rest of the day. That little message of unspoken grace had an electric effect. Drury could not now feel altogether alone in the world when he was on board the same ship as that girl with the soft sympathetic eyes and the marvellous hair. Next morning the potential bushranger appeared on deck shaved, if not quite in his right mind.

"Say, Drury," said the Californian, who was in a measure making this voyage for his health. A man with a double-barrelled shot gun was prospecting for him around his last known place of abode. "Seen the English girl?"

"What English girl? They are mostly American on board, it seems to me"—this with fairly well affected indifference.

"They may be mostly of any nationality they darn well please. Seen the girl?"

"'Seen' a lot of girls. Talk sense or don't bother me." This was said with an angry ring which told its own story.

"Gosh! You've took it sudden," the Californian commented carelessly, as he spat into the sea, and for the moment dismissed the matter from his mind. He had not meant the least offence, and his definition was apt, if inelegant. Drury had really no sensible excuse for his—aberration would not be too strong a word. He had just "took it." Of course he could plead that his case was not without precedent.

There was a concert in the saloon on the third evening out, and second-class passengers were invited. Miss Bute sang. She had only a drawing-room voice, but she sang with taste and feeling. What was more important, she recognised Drury as he could plainly see, before her glance was suddenly averted. That settled matters for him. He went back to his second class cabin greatly elated, and with a distinct conviction that various historical figures which have hitherto occupied high places in the common esteem were only very second-rate personages indeed. His ambition soared so very suddenly high, it is not surprising that, like a haughty spirit, it preceded a fall.

This fall was postponed for a few days by the force of circumstances. Drury was consequently enabled to go mooning about, fabricating delightful day-dreams in which he himself and the girl with the glorious hair were not merely the principal figures, but the whole *dramatis personae*. The day was not far distant when those two did really fill the bill in a very curious and not altogether delightful drama. But as the man was not a prophet, he could not foresee the troubles that were in store. He was thus for a time left to the comfortable possession of his ignorance.

At Honolulu, the usual contingent of globe trotters who had waited over from the previous vessel to see the great volcano, was shipped. The new arrivals constituted themselves a general nuisance for a day or two by their interminable descriptions of Kilauea, which, of course, was, at the moment of their inspection, in a particularly awful state of eruption. And their guide-book quotations about the "Paradise of the Pacific" were very wearisome to those who knew little of the Hawaiian group, and had no prospect of ever personally knowing more.

It was evening when the *Maori* steamed slowly out from Honolulu, and then, when the coral reef that guards the entrance to the harbour was passed, she went full speed and almost due south for Apia— another long spell of ocean travelling. Everybody was on deck to see the last of the land, and the new comers were all talking about it. They certainly could not have borne stronger testimony to the beauties of these lovely islands, where every prospect pleases and only man is—a little free and easy. The balmy airs that were always blowing; the summer seas that shimmered paradoxically in a place of perpetual spring; garlanded craigs, leaping cascades, plumy palms drowsing by the surf-beaten shore; the breath of flowers that was wafted many miles to sea, and so on *ad infinitum*. Then the ship's company settled down again to a homogeneous family with identical interests and common animosities.

It was a relief to the monotony of the voyage when a man called Smith—an Englishman—shot an albatross which had patiently followed the ship for many days. Smith was a member of a thirteen club, and fired the fatal shot under a strong sense of duty. His act was a merciful dispensation. It gave the people a new subject to contend over; so the poor albatross had not died in vain. Smith immediately took precedence of all passengers, ranking 'with, but after,' Miss Bute. His reading of the "Ancient Mariner" at one of the ship's functions was declared to be very vivid and realistic.

One morning, when Miss Bute was making her usual tour of the deck, she happened to walk, inadvertently, toward the second-class quarter. He was there, as in duty bound. She remained long enough to allow him to note the stylish cut of her tailor-made costume, and she glanced up toward a spar so that he could get a glimpse of her expressive blue eyes. Then she walked back to her own place, and let Drury feel that man was made to mourn.

"Fine girl, the Governor's daughter," the Californian remarked, again introducing that subject in the second-class smoke room. He had made his pile, he explained parenthetically (the man with the shot gun could have corroborated, had he been present), but was travelling cheaply from choice. Economy is a virtue which only the very poor despise. No one contradicted the man with the pile, so he continued:

"She's a darned first-rater. If I'd knowed she was aboard, I'd have travelled saloon. That's what I'd have done."

"Why would you have done that?" Drury asked coldly. "What difference would that have made?" He controlled his annoyance very well, but his voice shook a little.

"All the difference in the world. I'd have knowed her by this time. There! And what's more, my youthful friend, I'd have let her father know that I'm the best man on this ship. I could buy the whole show, passengers and all."

"You would have had to hurry up to tell him that," Drury snapped out.

"Not I. I have got my proofs, and I would have produced them under his own nose in his own stateroom. He could not dispute them."

"No, but he could have kicked you out of his room before your story was well begun—unless, as I said, you did the thing with a bit of a rush." This was the first time that Drury had spoken, as it were, above his breath. It made a sensation.

The Californian was thoughtful for a moment. He would have cheerfully shot a man for less. But the environment was not suitable. He spat and spoke:

"What'll you drink?"

"Nothing with you."

"The high horse seems to suit you."

Drury arose and went to the door of the room, in order to put an end to the conversation.

"Young, very young," the man with the money muttered, in a philosophical voice. "If I had him in Stonebroke Gulch I'd give him a lesson that would do him good." He added aloud, "Take my advice, young man, and stick to the Horse Marines. I mean, don't ride that horse of yours ashore. You'll be off before you know, if you do. That's straight?"

"He! he!" a nondescript traveller sniggered. His face had the characteristic weak points of half a dozen nationalities. "Good advice for a young man in love!"

When they got the nondescript upon his feet again, and picked the flakes of broken glass out of him, it was found that he was not very seriously injured by the force of Drury's remonstrance. This had taken a physical-force form—the line of least resistance with the average Briton.

"Guess I'll have to report you to the Captain," the Californian said, with a friendly wink, although so recently snubbed himself.

"When you like," Drury answered sulkily. His temper had completely mastered him. Remember that he was young, and that this was the first time he had been publicly charged with the offence. Thenceforth the

Governor's daughter was not referred to in the second-class smoke room.

Speeding south, every day brought bluer seas and balmier breezes. Soon the shipboard amusements were given up, and the *Maori's* people lay idly about in deck chairs, too indolent even to read. All through the long, bright days they were content to watch the lazy pacing clouds sailing on the bosom of the air, or to lean over the side and count the foam-flecked eddies of turquoise blue splashing past. All through the starry nights strange constellations were climbing the heavens or sinking in the dim horizon till they mingled with the phosphorescent track of the steamer, stretched like a terrestrial milky-way over the darkness of the ocean. Every morning the sun rose in a deeper flush of crimson; every evening he set in a richer halo of saffron. Day after day only the sea and the sky; the sky and the sea—magnificent, but rather monotonous!

One day the Governor's daughter wandered "forward" again. The bushranger was there, of course, on the same spot, just forward of the rail. He was permitted to look at her for three minutes; and had to live on that for forty-eight hours. Then, when Drury, who was now desperately lonely, second-class passenger too! It was unbelievable! With an insolent stare she turned away, taking the arm of a little Frenchman, who, Drury had noticed, was always dangling after her on deck, and who now came forward. The Frenchman accepted the compliment with the politeness of his country. His air of easy self-possession and confidence in his own priority to all males on the ship would have been an education to a student of the art of gallantry. It made Drury's brows gather together in an ugly horse-shoe which would have worked in well in the novel of a quarter of a century ago, and caused him to be very rude to a man for whom he was beginning to entertain a sincere respect.

"Have you heard the news?" the big German shouted in his excellent English as Drury dashed back into the smoking room he had so recently quitted.

"D—n the news!" Drury snapped, pushing past the other.

"Himmel! it doesn't need that. It is bad enough already."

"Then let's have it, and have it over."

"Very civil! You English always are civil when talking to foreigners? The German's brows went up and he shrugged his shoulders as expressively as if he had been of French extraction.

"Pardon me! No offence you know! What's the matter?" Drury asked a little more politely. He was vexed by the just judgment of the foreigner. But his own wound was too deep and too fresh to enable him to spare much sympathy. He wanted all his pity for himself.

"The barometer has fallen an inch in the last two hours."

"And what does that mean?"

"I know what it means off the coast of China, but I don't know what they call it hereabouts."

"What do they call it off the coast of China, then?"

The German puffed a little solemnly at his pipe and then said in a serious voice—

"Typhoon!"

Chapter II.
THE CRADLE OF THE DEEP.

THE sea began to rise before the wind came in earnest. As the evening wore on, the sky filled with masses of black, driving- clouds, of a ragged, oily appearance, behind whose dark fringes great streams of red and orange light, from a sinking sun, poured cataracts of colour. When the daylight died, and darkness swept over the ocean, the wind, which was very unsteady, increased in terrific gusts. By midnight the vessel was pitching and rolling in a very heavy sea. An hour later, the storm burst in its full strength. No one slept that night. The captain never left the bridge. Breakfast next morning was only for the few; the many had no stomach for it.

No change, except, if possible, for the worse, took place in the weather all day. The waves were immense, and the ship floundered over them and through them as helplessly as an amateur raft or a catamaran which had parted its outrigger. Then a tremendous sea swept over the vessel, carrying men, boats, and everything that was movable overboard. The engine-room was slightly flooded, which was serious; and two or three stokers disabled, which did not matter. What did matter was that something had evidently gone wrong with the machinery, for the speed of the ship was noticeably decreased. This was naturally a source of unlimited speculation amongst the passengers. They were very anxious to know what was at fault, and pressed the officers for information, which was courteously refused. It was not, however, long withheld. Before evening everything breakable on board had been smashed; several passengers were in hysterics, and most of the remainder too ill for nervous troubles. A general panic was, therefore, happily not to be feared—for the present. The diminished crew had quite enough to do, without being worried over the possible stampede of their human live-stock. The second night of the storm was worse than the first.

Most of the passengers endeavoured to introduce any topic of conversation, however *mal apropos*, just to show they were not afraid, or perhaps to occupy their minds in lieu of fear. In the second-class smoke room, Drury made quite an eloquent speech, of a very advanced order, as to politics, economics, and sociology generally. The argument was not so closely reasoned as one is accustomed to in the works of Mr. Herbert Spencer, but it had the merit of out-distancing Karl Marx in audacity.

The speaker was interrupted by a quiet man, a missionary, who having previously seen satisfactorily to the welfare of his soul, could afford to make light of the peril in which his body most certainly stood.

"So, young man, I gather that you do not favour the rights of property?"

"Not I," said Drury defiantly. His extempore address had created a digression which all admitted to be agreeable. The people were, therefore, in his debt. They would be lenient in their judgments.

"And that your ideas on property are merely founded on the fact that you haven't got any," the missionary pursued.

"Perhaps!" Drury agreed to keep the missionary going. The subject was certainly more cheerful than that of death by drowning.

"And would be modified if you had."

"Bravo, old man missionary!" the Californian exclaimed. "Got him this time, all the way."

Drury looked at the audience with a superior air and said quietly:

"Most certainly! The possession of a few trumpery toys or sparkling trinkets turns the best of us too soon into mere collectors —- or misers — or jackdaws.

"Himmel, it is one for our side!" the German shouted, waving his big-bowled pipe aloft.

But these efforts were as artificial as ephemeral. They dwindled away, and at last, in the saloons, the staterooms, the smokerooms, nothing but the weather and the quality of the ship were discussed. The most hardened jester had long since given over his joke about the "pacific" ocean, and all discussion on general subjects was abandoned. In the first saloon it ran thus:

"How far do you think we are from the Samoan islands, Sir William Bute? You have made this voyage before."

"I should say that, from the time we are out of Honolulu, we can't be more than 500 miles from Apia. I made the voyage once before, but I certainly did not experience anything in the way of a hurricane like this." Sir William spoke slowly, and in a rather ponderous way. He had found this method useful. By its assistance the most commonplace platitude had often done duty successfully for that marvellous intellectual power with which his friends accredited him—and which those who were not his friends marked "absent" from his discourses.

"Do you think there is—er—any danger?" the interviewer persisted.

Sir William glanced towards his daughter, and said, pointedly:

"Certainly not. The *Maori* is the newest ship on this route, and one of the best afloat. She is only a year old, and unsinkable. All the most modern—"

"All of which, papa, being for my benefit, we'll take as 'read.' What are the facts—I mean the odds? How much for or against the ship?" Miss Bute put in. It was plain that she knew the secret of Sir William's method.

"I wish you would not speak in that flippant way, Margery," the Governor replied. "We certainly are not in any immediate danger. But a storm like this is not to be laughed at."

"I am very much too seasick," Margery answered, "to laugh at anything, much less at a ship in distress when I am on board of it. But, as you say that we are in no immediate danger, there is no good in crying out. — Oh dear!"

This remonstrance was partly addressed to the *Maori*, which at the moment made an unseaworthy attempt to stand on her head.

"Pardon, Ma'am'selle," Alphonse Didot, the Frenchman, said politely. "You will be better in your stateroom. I will find your maid. Let me assist you."

"I will assist my daughter," Sir William interrupted loftily. As they retired in a sort of an Egyptian zig-zag, which did not show Sir William's bulky figure at its best, Alphonse grumbled angrily:

"Diable! One would think he was the only man in the world who had a daughter—which would be a misfortune! But this girl has taste and refinement, although English. She appreciates me."

As she left the saloon, Margery thanked M. Didot for his courtesy, with a glance which he accepted with becoming condescension.

In the second-class quarter consternation was fast degenerating into despair, and in the smoke room, which was now monopolised by the unmarried men, the conversation was far from unctuous.

"—, —, when the —, —-, —is this sort of thing to stop?" the Californian complained.

The German also commented suitably on the occasion.

"Say, Britisher"—from the Californian—"got nothing to add to what has fallen from Continental friend and self?"

"No. I think, between you, you've said all that's necessary. You have a talent for that kind of talk."

"Very sociable and perlite, I must say, and just what I would expect from an amiable young man like yourself."

"I don't mean to be rude," Drury protested; "but I can't always talk to you. You really tire me with your wealth of interjection, which our missionary friend would call blasphemous, but which I call ridiculous. I wish there was something for us to do. Anything would be better than this suspense."

"I'm with you there all the way, and if there's anything to be done, I don't reckon that you'll be backward in doing your share; and, darn me, but I'll stand in with you. I meant to shoot you first reasonable opportunity, but there's something straight about you I can't help liking. Shake!"

Drury gave his hand willingly, for the Californian, after all, was an unpretentious sort of rascal, and his cordial reply was unexpected. Just then a deafening crash of top-hamper falling on deck resounded over the ship as she pitched headlong into the trough of an enormous wave. The whole population of the vessel was now instantly in motion. Every individual made haste for the position where he could do most harm—that is, to hamper and distract those whose business it was to be on duty at that point. A serious deadlock was imminent. The crew were already shorthanded for the management of the ship. If the passengers broke altogether loose, then the last chapter in the story was already told.

Sullivan, the third officer of the *Maori*, a genial Irishman who looked upon life as just a long-drawn joke, dashed open the door of the second-class smoke room. The man seemed to have lost his own individuality. The terrible responsibility which rested on all the ship's officers had brought out the best that was in him. He was literally transformed. He shouted from the open door:

"Look here, you landlubbers. This ship's none so seaworthy at this particular moment as some of you may think, but don't tell that to the women; and we've lost a lot of our crew, and the passengers are going silly, and if they break loose the half of them will be in the azure main before they know where they are. I have no orders from the Captain, but I speak for myself. I think you and the men aft—the single men, the married men are busy looking after their own families—might do something better than sit there at your ease."

"What can we do?" George Drury shouted, as he jumped to his feet and held on by a table. The roar of the wind was terrible. It was hard to hear even one's nearest neighbour.

"That's like you, Drury. I expected it from you. You might manage amongst you to keep the passengers in order," Sullivan answered, and slammed the door to.

It was really a psychological moment. Drury rose to it. To mix the metaphor, it was the very hour for such a man. Physically brave, he was burning with the ambition to distinguish himself, in the hope of winning a girl's admiration. Here, surely, was a supreme crisis, in which he could stamp himself as of better clay than that of which the average man is moulded. His ostensible altruism, of course, was purely egoistic. But that's the way heroes are made, and on this occasion the heroism came in useful. Often it could be spared.

Drury steadied himself and cried out:

"Volunteers to preserve order on the ship!"

The second-class men answered manfully, and the first two to fall in were the Californian and the German.

To serve faithfully is "highly commended" in this world, and, we must believe, rewarded in the next. But to command wisely is no less praiseworthy, and one's reward, as it were, is payable in cash. Now Drury, we know, was a young man in a hurry. He was elected commander. That suited him.

Order forward was soon restored, or rather the frightened people were coerced into order. Then with a tramp remotely suggestive of that of drilled men, the volunteers marched aft, favoured not a little in their movement by a momentary steadiness of the *Maori*, now in the trough of a sea. Drury hailed the bridge.

"Hallo, Captain! We have restored order forward. If you will trust us with the charge of the passengers aft, you can then use your crew for their proper work."

"Who are you, sir?"

"George Drury—in command of the second-class volunteers."

"By whom are you appointed?"

"By the second-class volunteers."

The Captain thought for a moment and then called down:

"Very well, sir. I delegate to you and your men the charge of the saloon passengers as well as your own. I need every man that is left of my crew to work the ship." Captain Houston paused again for a second, and in that second, another green sea came aboard and a great cry arose from the lower deck fore and aft. Then Houston hailed Drury without further indecision:

"Below there! Batten down the passengers!"

"You shall not batten down me," Alphonse Didot said shortly. He was standing close to Drury, and heard the Captain's order. The truth is, he was desperately jealous of the second-class man's command. It might have been his, with all its honour and glory, if he had had the wit to think of it.

"You heard the Captain's order. Go below at once," Drury said quietly, but with the tone of command which had become habitual to him—in the last half hour. He had not, at the moment, any thought of jealousy.

"Not I! I am going to see this out on deck. *Voila!*"

"Below with you this moment, or you'll be thrown below."

"It will be unpleasant for the man who tries to throw me," Didot said, with an ugly smile which showed most of his white teeth. "When one travels with savages, one travels armed." He drew a revolver.

This might do in a stage play, but the issue was rather too serious for the introduction of melodramatic effects.

"Off with him. I'll ram his pistol down his throat if he tries to use it." Drury sprang on the recalcitrant passenger, and tore the revolver from his grasp. The pistol exploded twice, harmlessly, before the Frenchman was overpowered, kicked down the companion with emphasis and precision, and locked in his own stateroom.

While the saloon passengers were being got under hatches, the officer of the volunteer party felt a hand placed on his arm. He was about to wrest himself free, thinking it was some whimpering fool coming to him for advice or sympathy, when he saw that it was Miss Bute who detained him.

"You must go below with the others at once, Miss Bute." He spoke determinedly. He had really had a terrible time with the people, and his patience was giving out.

Margery's face was very white, but otherwise she appeared at ease. It flashed upon Drury that this girl, in spite of her superfine manner, was bearing herself with a quiet courage which made the conduct of many of the passengers appear contemptible, by way of contrast. The good impression which had thus been made was displaced immediately.

"Of course I am going below," Margery replied coldly. "I merely wished to thank you. I can appreciate what you are doing, and how well you are doing it. Besides I was—I was rude to you the other day, and I am very sorry." On that she turned away with the relieved air of one who has faithfully discharged a disagreeable duty, and extinguished an obligation by mentioning it.

For another hour there was no change, and then in a moment everything was altered by the worst mishap that can overtake a steamship at sea. A sudden shock was felt perceptibly all over the vessel. This was instantly followed by a grinding and crunching far below. When this, in turn, had stopped—it only lasted a second—the chief engineer rushed up from his room, hurried to the bridge, spoke a few words to the Captain, and then dashed back to the place from whence he came. Already the vessel's speed was noticeably slower—still slower—then it stopped dead. Without steerage way now, the *Maori's* head fell away, and she rolled broadside and nearly on her beam ends into the trough of an awful wave.

It was impossible to keep the news from the people. Among those on deck and those below who had any knowledge of the sea the word was passed from mouth to mouth, till every soul on board knew what the chief engineer had told the Captain: The shaft had broken!

Chapter III.
CLEAR AWAY THE BOATS.

FOR twenty hours the chief engineer and his men toiled at the broken shaft, without sleep and without food, save such as could be swallowed while they worked. During this time the passengers sank gradually into a pitiable condition. They knew that they were at sea on a sinking ship, in the middle of the Pacific Ocean, and the efforts made by the ship's officers to reassure them and to make light of the situation were utterly fruitless. It was the business of those in charge of the ship to sail her till she sank. Let them attend to that business. Their fugitive attempts to give heart to their passengers were at last resented as wearisome and inconsequent, and so they were discontinued. In sullen despair the people waited for the report of the chief engineer, who was working for all their lives. Everyone blamed him. It was his fault that the shaft was faulty, to begin with. Therefore, it was his fault that it broke. And he was taking an unconscionable time in mending a mere breakage—even if it were that of the shaft of an ocean liner at sea.

After superhuman labour, the shaft was almost repaired, when a message came from the Captain to the chief engineer. The engines must be started forthwith.

"Tell him I shall be ready in two hours."

The messenger went away, and returned quickly.

"He says you must start *now*."

"If we start now, the shaft will break again, and probably smash through the bottom of the ship. Tell him that," the chief engineer snapped, as with his own hand he gave the final blow to a rivet.

Once more the messenger returned.

"He says that the ship will capsize next big wave unless we get her head to the sea. The clinometer has twice shewn a heel of 45 degrees." On hearing this the chief engineer gave a few hurried directions, and went himself to see the Captain.

Captain Houston's face could hardly be seen under his sou'wester. The man seemed to be about half his ordinary size. He had dwindled into his wraps in a surprising way. The engineer spoke quickly, and gave his opinion that it was almost certain destruction to start under two hours.

"It is absolutely certain destruction to wait longer. I take the responsibility. You will start at once," the Captain answered.

"Say an hour, then!"

"You have your orders."

"But—-"

Houston went to his telegraph, and pushing the handle firmly down, rang to the engine room:

"Half speed ahead!"

"Give me your hand, sir," the Captain said to his engineer, as the latter was staggering off the bridge. The engineer had never felt the strain of his work till now, when all that he had done was to be sacrificed. And now he could hardly stand. His thoughts were naturally for the shaft, just as the Captain's were naturally for the ship.

"You've worked like a demon, Johnson, and I am sorry that I can't give you the time you want. Now go to your room and have a long sleep. You want it badly, and have earned it well. I seem to have lost the knack of it."

The terrible weariness in the last sentence struck the engineer in the right place. He shook his Captain's hand warmly, and remonstrated:

"Why don't you, too, go below, sir, for a spell. The shaft will stand some hours, at any rate. You can't even see the bow in this driving rain."

"No, I can't. But I can look that way," Houston answered shortly, pulling his sou'wester down.

"And you can do very little—"

"I can only do my best. Good-night, Johnson!"

The *Maori* came slowly round to the sea, and for a short time the terrified passengers felt a return of confidence, for the motion of the vessel, although still extreme, was now that of blissful rest after the fearful rolling they had experienced. But her progress under half steam was very slow, for a great deal of water had been shipped, and frightful head seas were bursting on her bows. This did not trouble Captain Houston. He was well content if he could only keep steerage way on her.

Another day of tempest was passed, and then, just as night fell, the engineer's prophecy was fulfilled. The hurriedly patched shaft broke again, and once more the *Maori* was at the mercy of the waves. It was, indeed, a night of terror. St. Elmo's fire, the sailors' "deadman's lights," tipped the masts and festooned the shattered shrouds. Enormous seas broke over the ship, and deluged her from stem to stern. Every roll sent her almost on her beam ends, and once every soul on board thought she had gone over. All hope of the vessel riding out the storm had to be abandoned, and when she was as full of water from the seas she had shipped as Houston deemed she could hold and float, he hardened his heart, and gave the last order to which a good captain consents:

"Clear away the boats! Hands to stations!"

All the boats which were still sound had been previously made ready as far as possible, and fresh crews told off for them. The number of boats which had been stove in, and the number of men who had been lost, rendered rearrangement necessary. The last preparations were soon completed, and all were ready to quit the ship. The volunteers had now their hands very full, for the Captain had given them complete control of the passengers, while his diminished and exhausted crew got out the boats. Drury spoke to the passengers earnestly, and, indeed, with something still of the masterful ring in his voice which the sudden responsibility of command had raised in it—a responsibility which, it was evident, was to be as brief as it was unexpected, and which must surely soon be ended by the death of all concerned. The people, first as well as second-class, listened carefully to him, for the Pacific Ocean is no respecter of persons, and this youth had shewn that he had good judgment as well as a stout heart. But when the first lifeboat was got over the lee side, an ugly rush was made for it.

"Keep back, there!" Houston shouted from the bridge, and his voice could be distinctly heard above the roar of the storm. "Women and children first!"

A man distraught with terror—the nondescript of no particular nationality—dashed forward. He was thrown back violently by the guard under Drury. He dashed on again.

"Let him go this time" was roared from the bridge. The man sprang again toward the boat. A little smack, hardly audible in the raging chorus of wind and wave, sounded on the bridge. A puff of smoke followed, and the man went over the side with a bullet in his brain.

"To let the others know," Houston shouted, "that this is a British ship!"

After that stern lesson, the people maintained good order and bore themselves bravely.

Everything was done decently and according to regulation. Each crew got their own boat swung out and lowered to the ship's rail—two men looking after the tackles. Then the boat was filled as full as was safe with crew and passengers, and let down into the sea. A few followed by the rope ladders and some were desperate enough to jump into the water on the chance of being picked up. Several were lost in this perilous leap for life; others were dragged on board the boat they tried for. And so on, until the last boat was hanging on the davits. It had to be lowered into the sea by its own crew. They took the "falls" into the boat with them, and it was soon level with the rail. Two men only were now left on board—Captain Houston and George Drury. Houston pointed to the boat. He himself must be the last to leave his own ship. Drury stepped in at once. The Captain followed, and the boat instantly began to descend. A cry of anguish sounded over the water. It was from Sir William Bute. He was in the last boat which had been launched—the last but one which left the ship.

"My daughter is still on board."

Two men sprang to the ropes. One, Alphonse Didot, missed his grasp and stumbled. He went over the side before a hand could be raised to help him, and disappeared without a cry in the sea. The other, George Drury, was more fortunate. He clambered on board, and shouted back to Captain Houston as he gained the deck:

"For God's sake wait a minute for me, Captain. You said I served you well. I claim a minute."

"Lower away," the Captain commanded. "We'll be dashed to pieces against the ship's side."

"I claim a minute," Drury cried. "If I am not back in that, you can go without me—and without dishonour."

"It is risking the lives of every soul on board this boat," the Captain answered. "But I give you five minutes! If you are not back then I will cast off; and once I have done so, I will not put back for you—not if you were my own son."

"I hold you to your promise!"

Drury ran to the saloon companion, and sprang down it, several steps at every bound. And now came a difficulty which he must have foreseen had a moment's reflection been allowed him. Miss Bute must be lying ill in her stateroom, or she would have left the ship with the first of the women. Drury remembered seeing her maid passed into a boat, and thought there was something not very convincing in her manner when she was questioned by Sir William Bute about her mistress. The girl replied that her mistress was in the first boat, but it was now plain that in her terror she gave the readiest answer which came to her, or the one which would cause the least delay. Sir William had broken down under the severity of the ship's pitching, and had to be assisted on deck. Hence his ignorance of his daughter's position. The maid's conscience had probably stung her at the last moment. Where, now, was Miss Bute's stateroom? How was it to be found in the five minutes' grace? Not by idle speculation, at any rate. One minute was already wasted!

Drury dashed blindly forward, for the ship was almost in darkness, only lit, indeed, by a few oil lamps, which no one had taken the trouble to put out—the electric lighting had broken down early in the gale. He called loudly as he ran along the corridors. He could not have opened all the doors in the time, much less have examined the compartments. Indeed, the doors were already all open, as they had been left by their late occupiers—all save one. This must be hers. But it was locked or fastened on the inside, and two minutes were gone.

The door would not yield, although Drury threw himself against it with all his force. If he had only a weapon of any sort! But there was no time to look for one—and the third minute hastened furiously past. In an effort of sheer despair he dashed his body once more against the wood-work. The lock gave, and the door was burst open so suddenly that he fell headlong into the stateroom.

Miss Bute was lying, fully dressed, in her berth. She had probably fainted at the last moment. At least she was now unconscious. Drury caught her up in his arms, and hurried back to the deck. But the light was bad, and twice, in his desperate haste and with the violent motion of the ship, he stumbled, and he knew he must move more carefully if he meant to reach the side at all. He did reach the side at last, and deserved better of fortune. For, alas! when he got there the five minutes were up.

"Help! help! I have got the girl. See here! Don't leave us, Captain Houston. Don't run away!"

"It is the almost certain loss of the lives of twenty for the chance of saving two," Captain Houston said to himself. He was about to give his final order when the Californian arose, and, holding on by the burly German with one hand, while he put the other to his mouth by way of a speaking tube, yelled out:

"Drop the dead woman and jump. Darned if we don't pick you up somehow. You've got grit, and I've got a gun as well as the others, and I am not goin' to see you left. I'll do some shootin' first."

"Gott! that is well said," the German assented.

"If that man draws a pistol," Houston cried to his men, "throw him overboard. We'll stand by for a minute, all the same."

The phrases which come so glibly to a lover's lips about dying cheerfully for his mistress are surely, sometimes, not altogether honest. And certainly very few civilized human beings will voluntarily give up their own lives as a sentimental sacrifice to the already dead. So Drury turned with a gasp to the inanimate bundle which hung so limply in his arms, as this last glimpse of possible life was flashed to him. But she was not dead. She breathed. His chance of life was gone. Laying her gently on the deck, he leaned over the rail and shouted:

"The girl is not dead. I will not desert her. Save yourselves."

"Don't be a fool," the Captain shouted back "Jump for your life and—"

Houston's words were cut short. A great wave broke over the *Maori's* stern, and swirling up on the lee side of the ship, plunged over the boat in a foaming smother which nothing of her size could stand. All was over in a second. Not a man was saved, or even seen by the horrified watcher on deck, and it was only for a moment that he had a glimpse of the capsized boat as it drifted off.

Chapter IV.
ALONE!

GEORGE DRURY turned from the side with a muttered exclamation, on the entry for which I trust the recording angel has dropped a tear. Then raising the still unconscious girl in his arms, he staggered back to the saloon. A ladies' cabin opened off this, and hither he brought her and laid her gently on a couch. It were better that she should not awake—should never awake from this strange sleep or swoon. He brought in the last oil lamp, which was still burning; also a large carving knife which he found on one of the saloon tables. It was the only deadly instrument he could lay hands upon, and he did not know what might yet happen, or for what purpose he might have to use it. When the whole situation began to unfold itself fully to his agitated mind, he asked himself had he not been rather foolish, if not entirely a fool, for declining at the last moment to leap overboard—even if he carried the girl with him. His momentary delay had probably sacrificed the lives of all in the last boat which left the ship. Of course they would most likely have gone to the bottom ten minutes or half an hour later. That did not justify him. And all had been done for a girl who had never spoken a really civil word to him; who had once looked very insolently at him; and only once or twice the other way! To attempt to save her was his plain duty. To elect deliberately to perish with her seemed, just then, rather quixotic. But what had passed could not be helped, so he dismissed it, although with an effort.

Margery still breathed softly. If her chance of life under the circumstances was a poor one, at least she was not yet dead. Drury looked about for something which might happily revive her, and found several water jugs lying about, all empty, and the fragments of many more. Then he discovered something more useful—an unbroken and unopened soda water bottle. There was no corkscrew, so he broke off the neck of the bottle and splashed its contents over the girl's face, chafing her hands vigorously. For a long time there was no result. When animation at last returned to his patient, it was with a suddenness which was rather startling. She moaned once or twice, sighed deeply, sat up and asked him an embarrassing set of questions.

"Why am I here? Why are you here? What has happened?" She asked all three questions in the same breath, without waiting for an answer to any one of them.

He prevaricated with the best intention, but she interrupted him.

"What has happened?" she asked sharply.

"Oh, a great deal—of which I will tell you when you allow me to speak."

"But where are the ladies? How is it that you are here—in this cabin? You are—?"

"I am—a second-class passenger."

"I know that. I remember you very well. Who are you? I mean, what is your name?"

"You ask two questions. I will take them in order" (he was talking against time). "Firstly: Who am I? Nobody! Secondly: What is my name? George Drury. That conveys nothing to you. In fact it means nothing. I had intended that one day it should mean something. But events have forestalled me. It doesn't matter. Then as to another brace of questions—as to why I am in this cabin, and where the ladies are—"

"Yes, I also asked that. It's all so mysterious—so inexplicable."

"I was about to explain it all when you interrupted me. You have been very ill—"

"Where, then, is my father?"

Drury made a gesture of pretended annoyance, and said, in the hardest voice he could command:

"I really think you had better tell the story yourself. You pull me up so short."

"Go on, then. But please explain quickly. I—I—am not very well yet. Forgive my impatience."

There was nothing else for it. In common justice to one who was so soon to walk with him through the valley of the dark shadow, he must no longer flinch. Drury began very seriously:

"When I broke into your stateroom you had fainted-"

"When you broke into my stateroom!" Her scornful tone was hard to bear; hard for a man who had tried so hard to save her.

"Yes, I broke into your stateroom, else you would still be there, and I would not be here." This was said quietly, but his voice grew somewhat bitter as he continued, using the same words once more:

"When I broke into your stateroom I found that you had fainted. And so you did not hear the preparations?"

"The preparations! What preparations?"

"The preparations—for quitting the ship!"

Overhead the thunder of the seas dashing over the vessel and the noise of the wind never slackened. The girl stopped, quite stunned for a moment. Contrasted with the silence of the cabin, the sound and fury without was very terrible. She sprang to her feet crying out:

"The ship must then be sinking!"

"I fear it is."

"And you sit here, talking to me like an old nurse, when in the hurry of the moment we may well be forgotten!"

Her strength was almost gone, but she struggled up from the couch and staggered toward the door. He stopped her, before she reached it.

"Would you murder me?" she gasped, as he forced her gently back to the couch. "We may be left behind."

"No fear of that!"

"Then in mercy let me go—and—come yourself."

"It is now too late."

Her eyes were hard to meet. He must get through with this, so he said, in a low but clear voice:

"We are left behind."

"Have you arranged that?" The girl was now plainly hysterical, so the wild accusation, cruelly unjust as it was, must not be judged too harshly. Drury took no immediate notice of it, for he knew very well that his companion was not responsible, at the time, for anything she might say or do. After a minute or two he spoke, and when he did he remembered that a little firmness is desirable in dealing with a hysterical patient.

"I may say that I did arrange this business as to a small detail," he said very calmly. "That is, I arranged for my own presence here. I certainly might have gone in the last boat." He did not tell her that the last boat had gone to the bottom for her sake. "Indeed, the last boat waited, on the Captain's word of honour, five minutes for me; but the door of your room was hard to break, and the time was up when I got you to the side, and the boat was launched." He paused to give her time to think, and then went on remorselessly, in the hope of stinging her brain into normal activity, and certainly with no thought of his own vainglory.

"I might, even then, have left you, for a man cried out to me to drop you and swim for it. But, you see I didn't. That's why I am here. That's how I have arranged everything, as you say."

At this, which might well have touched her, was partly lost on the girl, for the simple reason that, in the whirl of events since her senses returned, she was so overwhelmed that she could have hardly told her own name. Once, in the tossing of the ship, she was flung violently from the couch. Drury snatched her up, and put his arm round her gently to keep her on the seat. She did not speak, but automatically shrank back. He drew his arm away instantly. They sat thus for some hours without many words.

Margery's splendid hair had been released from its fastenings by the wind on that double deck journey when Drury carried her. It now hung down her back like a school girl's. She made no attempt to re-coil it, and did not even seem to notice it. As she leant forward, her hands clasped tightly on her knees, her brows knotted in an effort to think, the great coils fell forward till they almost hid her face. She flung them back once or twice by an impatient movement of her head, and resumed her brooding. In the dim light of the fast expiring lamp she was a strange, almost a weird, picture. Drury did not speak. She would puzzle out the problem better, he thought, without his help. In pity for her he forgot his own pain, and he forgave her his danger out of a compassion which was soon to be very freely drawn on.

At last the girl made a great effort and said, "I really cannot explain. I have been ill, and the doctor made me up a bottle of medicine to get me some sleep, and whether he made it stronger than he intended, or labelled it wrongly, or that I mistook the directions, I cannot say. But I am absolutely stupefied. I don't rightly know what has happened. If I have said anything to pain you, perhaps you will forgive me—"

"Don't say another word. I am not altogether a brute. Rest a little. You will need all your strength by and bye."

"You forgive me," she murmured, with a little sob.

"Oh, yes, I forgive you—that is, I would forgive, only there is not anything to forgive. You may sleep now. I will call you if any change comes."

She nestled on the couch, for the drug she had taken was again overpowering her, and rested her head on her arm cosily. She was just falling asleep when an immense wave struck the ship, and seemed to lift it bodily into the air. Then the vessel plunged forward on her smothered bows, and the whole fabric plunged down. Simultaneously a tremendous body of water swept over the deck above, so heavy that the *Maori* shook under the great weight.

Margery sprang from her couch and shrieked aloud. Drury was by her side in a moment. This time his supporting arm was not resisted. He kissed her on the forehead, and said:

"Be very brave for a little. It will not be long now."

The howling of the wind ceased suddenly. The vessel was quite steady now, riding on an even keel. But the sickening sensation of sinking down continued.

"What has happened?" the girl cried.

"I—do not know!"

"You know quite well. I think I know, too. You are a man. It is your place—your duty—to speak."

"I think the vessel is under the surface now."

"And—?"

"We are going down!"

Chapter V.
IN THE DEPTHS OF THE SEA.

"HOW long the water keeps out!" Margery cried, with a moan.

"It is probably the imprisoned air which is keeping it out. It will break in when the pressure is sufficiently increased by the depth. As well that as slow suffocation! Far better, indeed!" Drury answered, almost indifferently. The man was mentally stunned. He was unable to think normally. Their hushed voices sounded audibly in the cabin. No sound from without now interfered with any sound within.

"Let me hold your hand," Margery whispered. All reserve between them was over. What did it now signify whose fault it was that they were together in such a terrible extremity? All that now mattered was to face the end as bravely as possible, with the courage of despair.

"I—I—do not think I was ever much of a coward," Margery Bute said slowly. "But I never thought I should have to face a death like this. And you—you don't even seem to care—" She stopped short with a piteous gesture.

The oil lamp burned lower still. The air, then, was giving out.

"You are bearing up well," Drury urged. "Be brave to the end. Don't break down now. It would do no good. I am sorry for you; you have so much to lose. You have everything to lose that makes life worth living. I have nothing of any consequence to part from. It is not so hard for me." He hardly knew what he was saying. But he must talk. He must help her till the end.

Margery did not altogether break down. She was thoroughbred in the real as well as in the conventional meaning of the word. Her courage came and went fitfully, it is true; but mostly it was on the right side.

"How long do you think it will be till—till the water breaks in?" she asked, with dry lips. That question was always forcing itself upon them.

"I do not know. I do not know at what rate the ship is sinking, and if I did, I have not the technical knowledge to calculate the time. What does it matter?" They did not speak again for a little while, but just waited—and waited—and waited!

There was a sudden grating sound below, then a great shock came, and the motion of the vessel, of which they were still partly conscious, ceased. The ship heeled over, recovered slightly, and rested firm.

"This is the end!" the girl gasped.

"Yes, the ship is now at rest—at the—at the bottom of the sea! Give me your other hand."

"Just a word! For pity's sake believe it. I thought you had tricked me at the risk of my life. I see now that you tried to save it at the then possible and now certain cost of your own. I am sorry. That is all; but you believe me. Answer quickly, before it is too late."

"Yes; I believe you."

She let her head sink upon his shoulder, murmuring, "How long—how long the water keeps out. It is becoming harder to bear, this terrible suspense. Ah! It is unbearable! God in heaven have mercy on us, and kill us and be done with it!" She started up with a wild cry, but he restrained her.

"Hush! Hush! That will do no good. Put down your head again. There! There! Let us die together—that way!"

"In the depths of the sea!" Margery sobbed, "In the depths of the sea!"

Drury touched her cheek gently with his own and whispered:

"Courage! It will soon be over now."

And still the water kept out. And the old Reaper kept on sharpening his scythe and would not strike.

Margery sank again into a state of coma. The tension was too great. Her nervous system, deranged as it had been by the overdose of the drug, broke down under the fearful strain. She could feel no longer. George Drury, now alone—for the girl was quite unconscious—held on firmly in his great fight with fear. He would not give in. He would face death when it came to him with a stout heart. He would not cry out until he was hurt—nor even then. But the air was becoming suffocating. He breathed with difficulty. They would be slowly tortured to death as the air gave out. The horrors of the Black Hole of Calcutta came to his mind. That long agony would be theirs. The girl he had tried so hard to save would be gradually done to death, and he would not be able to raise a hand to help her. She would awake and beg him to kill her and put her out of her agony, and he would not have the strength to do it then. A terrible thought possessed him. He would not have the strength then, but he had the strength now! He wrestled fiercely with, the thought. A hoarse voice that he hardly knew to be his own rang through the cabin, "I cannot do it!" This was followed by "God have mercy on me, I must!" Great drops of sweat broke on his forehead.

The struggle was very terrible. It was over at last; he would do what he thought was right. She might awake at any moment; it must be done quickly. He would kill her first and then himself; for the water would never come in—not until they were long past its spite. He must find a weapon. The knife! Yes, the knife would serve very well.

The oil lamp flickered and went out. The darkness which followed was absolute; its intensity was appalling. For a minute or two Drury sat irresolute. After all should he not try to arouse her and give her a little time to prepare for death. Her sleep now seemed almost natural. She breathed regularly. But then, would it be a real kindness or only a savage cruelty to awake her? Surely cruelty! He would kill her, then, while she slept. Having come to his final decision, he prepared to perform it without shrinking. It was an awful crime, looked at in one way; a merciful act of grace in another. His conscience did not reproach him, but his nervous system required a strong current from the brain to keep its qualms under. He would not allow it to disturb his purpose, for his purpose was right. This lad of fads and theories had developed fast in the stress of the events he had undergone. He was a practical man now—a surgeon or a butcher, according to your point of view. There is such a wealth of difference in different points of view.

Drury tried the temper of the knife, and then its edge and point. It was one of those great carving knives which are as keen almost as a razor, and as stout as a bayonet. The knife satisfied him, careful as he was that no avoidable suffering should be caused. He put his hand on the girl's neck and found that her tightly buttoned dress covered her throat where he intended to strike. It resisted his fingers. He had neither time nor patience to unfasten it. So he slipped the point of the knife below it, and with a long tearing "zip," the cloth gave way before the keen edge. If he had only had a pistol, like the others. With that you just pull the trigger, and the rest you cannot help. But the knife is a brutal weapon. And it was such a soft and slender throat! He might even yet have paused, only that nothing now appealed to him, save the craving to get the thing over and be done with it. He would have less compassion in his own case. Just before he would draw the knife across the girl's throat, he pulled out his watch in a mechanical way to see the exact moment of her death. Then he found he had not another match. He groped for the knife he had laid down, and was about to replace his watch, when he looked automatically at the dial. A miracle! He was so highly strung, that even in the intense darkness he imagined he could distinguish the face of the watch in his hand. Delusion! He looked steadily at it—glared at it! Yes, there was a little disc whiter, or less black, than everything else in that dreadful nocturne.

"It is surely a delusion," Drury gasped. Still he glared steadily at the disc, or where he thought the disc was. He moved his hand to and fro. The little grey circle moved with the motion of his arm. Now close to his eyes—now at arm's length! He forgot the knife. Then this mirage, or madness, strengthened slowly, rather than diminished. Minutes passed, and still he glared at the grey disc. He thought he could see black splashes where the figures marking the hours should be. These strengthened, became blacker, more distinct. At last, two little lines, ghostly shadows, began to stretch across the grey circle which his imagination had conjured up, and was trying hard to compel him to believe was the face of his watch. One of the little lines of shadow moved slowly round. Then the black splashes grew clearer still, and the little lines less shadowy. And at last the man's heart throbbed violently, and then seemed to stop. For he knew now that he was not deceived.

He had seen light!

It was true. The deck-light above his head showed a little circumference less black than all around. Drury opened the cabin door and made his way through the still darkened saloon. Then, after a few steps, a fortune beyond the dreams of avarice was in his grasp—-air, light, life itself, all came to him with the coming dawn. There is no dawn in the depths of the sea. Therefore the ship was still above water. He dashed up the companion, shouting aloud in his great joy. The *Maori* was really on the bottom of the sea, but happily the sea was not very deep at the place. She was high and dry in a long, rock-bound lagoon. She had drifted into it over the angry churn of two opposing currents, which meet at its entrance and form a terrible bar. This had lifted the vessel bodily up, as her two passengers remembered, deluged her with raging billows, and then flung her headlong into her haven. Here she was beached in perfect safety, her starboard side resting against a gigantic cliff, which rose sheer from the water of the lagoon. The failing air, which Drury had fancied suffocating, was only the change from the gale of the roaring forties to the perfect calm of the rock-bound sea. But, in his condition of mind, it is no wonder that he mistook the stuffy cabin, poisoned as it was with the fumes from an ill-trimmed and improvised oil lamp, for a death trap. The crunch of the *Maori*, self-beached, passed easily for the last resting of the ship on the bottom of the sea, a hundred fathoms deep.

"Come on deck! Come on deck!" Drury cried, hysterically, as he rushed back to the cabin. "It is all a dreadful nightmare, Miss Bute, that you have had. We are alive and well, and not at the bottom of the sea. Lean on me. You are very weak still."

"My father—?" Margery murmured, still half asleep.

"I trust is well. This way, the fresh air will soon revive you."

Margery did not appear to notice the deserted saloon, the absence of crew and passengers. Her brain was again clouded. She had mercifully forgotten the misery of the previous night. When they gained the deck, she looked around amazed. She was trying hard to think out the puzzle. Drury interfered, and blundered. He commenced with great enthusiasm:

"You remember their leaving the ship?"

"No. I think you told me of that."

"But you remember afterwards when I—when I told you we were at the bottom of the sea?"

"Yes, I am beginning to remember things. I remember that very well."

"And now you see we are on dry land."

She totally mistook his perhaps ill-timed attempt at raillery. She was not really responsible for what she said. Her brain was still partly paralysed. Besides, the situation, as she found it, was enough to confuse the strongest mind.

"I do not understand what has happened. I am absolutely mystified as to everything save one, which is that you have lied to me magnificently. You nearly drove me mad last night with your story of the ship being under water, and your mock heroics about facing death, which from your triumphant manner now, I can see that you considered a splendid joke. I don't see anything very splendid in it. It was heartless."

"I certainly was not joking," Drury said, coldly, "when I told you the ship was under water, for I believed it myself."

"Bah! I suppose you believe this island is under water? What a dreadful mystery everything is!" Margery cried, passionately. She crossed the deck hastily to where Drury stood in what he meant for a stately, but which may have only been a melodramatic, attitude. She looked him squarely in the face and said: "This is the second time I am bewildered. I do not know what to believe. Have you mesmerised me?"

He answered very bitterly—for this was a poor reward for all he had done and suffered—"I believe I have. I found you only a rather vain, and, so far as I knew, not a particularly amiable girl. And I have turned you into—this!"

He shrugged his shoulders and left her without another word.

Chapter VI.
DUTY.

AS Drury strode off indignant, he heard a sharp exclamation, and faced round. Margery was looking at him with an expression which may be passed over without description, seeing that she was entirely in error as to the cause of her present discomfiture. The wind had fallen almost to nothing, but it had changed, and blew right up the lagoon. This morning breeze had breathed upon the ship and its two passengers. It stirred the girl's disordered hair and fanned her feverish brow. Alas! it also disturbed her mangled dress.

Margery was nearly always picturesque in her postures, which were sometimes unconscious, if more often intentional. She had certainly never been more picturesque than at this moment when standing on the deck of the *Maori*—her splendid hair blowing round her handsome and interesting, if rather diminutive face, in a warm toned aureola that shimmered in the rays of the morning sun; her eyes ablaze; her bosom heaving: when by a single look she challenged the only other human being, so far as she knew, within a thousand miles anywhere in the four points of the compass. Her challenge was answered at once, and in a way that surprised her. The culprit immediately pleaded guilty. But he did so in a cool, unapologetic way that was disquieting.

"Yes, I did that—in the cabin last night, while you were asleep or unconscious." This was said with a calmness that was almost stolid.

"You—you cad!"

The red dashed over the girl's face in a painful rush.

"You mistake." Drury's eyes flashed, but he went on smoothly, as if answering a civil question. "I—I was in a position of desperate difficulty, and I had come to a very terrible decision, which was entirely in your interest, as I believed at the time. I mean that I was acting, as I thought, in mercy to you. I will not describe my dilemma for two reasons: one is, that the action I had decided upon it too terrible to mention to you; the other is, that you probably would not believe me." He earnestly hoped she would contradict this.

"You are right," she interrupted, stamping her foot upon the deck; "I would not believe you."

"Then there is no more to be said. That ends all sympathy between us." Drury spoke very quietly, but

Margery's face turned white at his words, notwithstanding all the dangers she had passed.

Meantime, Drury went on in a cold but studiously courteous voice, and with a trace of his old academic style, which he might have avoided under all the circumstances. "We are in an extremely difficult, probably desperate, position. It is necessary, for whatever chance of life may remain to us, that there should be no divided counsels. We must both act for our mutual welfare. To insure that there will be no dissension I now take command. You shall obey."

"If I do not obey?"

"I will compel you—that is all. In primitive communities there is only one law—that of the strongest." (Adam Smith, the evil that you have done lives after you.—ED.) "Ours is a very primitive community, a community of two, and I am the stronger. Is not that enough?"

"Not altogether!" Margery's white face now took upon it a new look of resolution that was very foreign to it. "I did not, of course, expect the speech of a true gentleman from you, nor even that of a merely conventional gentleman—"

"Perhaps it is just as well, considering everything, that I am not a merely conventional gentleman," Drury said in a low voice, not meant for the girl's ear. But she heard him.

"At least you need not be unmanly."

"I shall endeavour not to be. What is more, I don't think I have been, so far as you are concerned."

She was fingering at her belt in a nervous way, so Drury added, with a hard, sarcastic ring in his voice:

"I really hope you have not a revolver there. The *Maori* people were surely the most warlike ship's company that ever put to sea. We have had enough of that."

"It isn't a pistol. If it were, I think you would mend your manners very soon."

"Not at all. I should just take it from you as I took one from your friend, Jean Jacques, or whatever his name was—. I am sorry I said that, as he is dead now." The sarcastic note was absent from the last remark.

"He's what?"

Poor Margery! It was no wonder that she did not know what to believe or disbelieve, or whether the whole horrible medley was not the result of mesmerism or hypnotism, or some similar "ism" as powerful and detestable as either. She was hardly shocked by what she now heard—just a little more puzzled than ever. She had lost, for the time, the capacity of being shocked.

"Drowned," Drury continued, less stiffly. "He and I made a jump together for the deck of the *Maori*, when your father called out that you had been left behind. He missed and I caught. One was taken and the other left. Quite scriptural, isn't it? Only that the right one was taken and the wrong one left; which is hard upon you, but my fortune—I mean misfortune—rather than my fault. We won't discuss that, however. I must now only remember that you are a helpless girl—"

"I am not so helpless as you think. I am not afraid of you." If he could only have used a little more tact—with all his advanced ideas and fine ideals! Or if Margery could only have fully believed him, they would have spared each other much unhappiness.

"I sincerely hope you are not. I trust that you will rely on me to protect you to the very best of my power, and that you will find that I am only anxious you should be as much at ease as in your own drawing-room in London. At the same time, this is hardly the time or place to brag about one's sense of security. Your want of trust in me neither enhances your safety nor lessens it. I will do what

I can to help you, but, of course, after this there can, as I have said, be no sympathy, much less friendship, between us."

These words fell with a cold chill upon poor Margery's emotional heart. She was enraged, defiant, and utterly rebellious, for she had been most grievously insulted in a hateful personal way. Yet this cool summing up of the case, and utter absence of regret, did not please her well, notwithstanding her own disclaimers. She did not really care an iota whether she ever saw him again in the world, once they were safely off the island and back to civilization—so she said to herself. But it was rather impertinent in him not to care, or to care so little. His complete indifference did not soften her temper.

The sun was now well over the horizon, and the vast rollers of the Pacific, which could be seen beyond the bar, were burnished by the golden rays. Inland, the wonderful foliage of the tropical island was gorgeous in its splendid greenery. Gaudy-plumaged birds began to flit from tree to tree, and insects hummed on busy wing in the summer air. Deep down in the clear water, where the ship was lying on a firm bed, beautiful groves of white, and red, and brown, and green coral could be seen quite clearly. Through these ocean woods vast swarms of multi-coloured fish—yellow, blue, scarlet, gold, and violet, some chastely clad in the primal hues of the rainbow, some streaked and spotted, harlequins of the deep—were dashing hither and thither. Great crabs sidled along. The sea anemones spread long feelers for their prey. All nature was up and awake, singing a matinee of motion, colour, and life.

"Better go to your own stateroom now and rest," Drury began in a somewhat kinder voice, for the great beauty of the scene had a strangely soothing influence. "I have much to think about, much to arrange. For instance, I must examine the condition of the vessel, as well as I can, considering that I have absolutely no technical knowledge. With all this you have nothing to do. Besides, under all the circumstances which have passed, in some of which you were unconscious, and others which you have misjudged, it may be more satisfactory if we remain better strangers until a passing ship relieves us of each other's company."

Margery glanced at him swiftly, and not apparently relishing the expression of his face, went to her stateroom as she had been requested. Drury left the ship by a rope ladder, which he made fast to a boat davit, and floating himself on a log to a little bay, formed by a gap in the cliff, about twenty yards away, he clambered up the rocks and soon disappeared among the palms and orange trees which, with their great festoons of parasitic creepers, covered the island. He took with him the sporting rifle which the thirteen-club man had left behind, and a liberal supply of cartridges. The island was so small it was most unlikely to be inhabited, but other dangers might be met with, and it was better to be sure than sorry.

The lady of the ship returned to the deck in time to watch the receding figure until it was hidden by the distant palms. Then she stood for a moment looking seawards, where, through the narrow entrance to the lagoon, she could see the blue shimmer of the ocean. When the minute was up, the yearning look left her wet eyes and her features hardened. Escape was impossible, quite, so there was nothing to be gained by crying over it. She could not help hoping for it, of course, but meantime she would do her duty. Besides the doing of it would be the best, as it was the only distraction left to her. She left the deck again and went below, this time to the saloon.

The girl—in spite of her resolve to be firm, which had a tendency to slacken when she did not guard it—did not go below to idle. She began work at once, but before doing so she bound up her abundant hair, and made some changes in her dress, which while simplifying its appearance, she was careful did not render it less attractive. Single-handed as she was, the task of clearing out the whole debris in the saloon was hopeless, and was at once abandoned. She gave up all thought of that on seeing how complete the chaos was; but she managed to cover up the remains of the last meal the passengers of the *Maori* had tried to eat, and hide them under a tarpaulin of table linen. The place was certainly not much bettered by this, but it did not look so dreadfully dreary. It was not so unsightly. Then she carried up some plates and cups, and bread and fruit, with a small bottle of wine, and such other things as could be most easily found lying about, and laid a dainty breakfast-table in the music room. This was already partly dried by the strong rays of the sun, and was bright and cheerful compared with the sodden saloon. A "dainty" table may be thought an euphemism, but it really was very prettily set out, for Margery had always been a capital executive at picnics, improvised yachting parties, and all sorts of social emergency meetings. The glass was polished till it shone; the napkins were folded smartly—a pretty trick of hers; and out of pure devilment—for there was a good deal of temper in the whole scheme—the chairs were turned up, marking the table "engaged." She had found a spirit-lamp, and prepared coffee hastily. The master of the ship was now visible on his way back.

Drury delivered his report the moment he stepped on deck. He was tired and hot, and so cut it short. The island, so far as he could see, was uninhabited. It was such a speck in mid-ocean there was no possibility, he thought, that it could be inhabited. There was, therefore, little more to be said, and absolutely nothing to be done.

"There's something; there's breakfast," Margery said, a little coldly, perhaps, considering all the trouble she had taken.

"Where, in the name of wonder? I thought we should have to forage for it!"

"In the music room. I have foraged for it. This way, please." Her face was a riddle which Drury could not read.

When the tired explorer saw the comfortable meal which awaited him, his heart, manlike, softened, and he would have said a mumbling word of gratitude had not Margery intervened.

"No thanks, please! This is my department."

In the excess of her pretended humiliation, she made as if she would wait at table, but this he had the common sense not to notice. He simply remained standing until she had taken her seat. The breakfast was quite as good as it looked, and that was very good. Conversation at table was rather limited, and what there was of it was not quite candid on either side. But it improved as it went on, and before the meal was over it had become conventional. Plates, cups, etc., were handed about with the usual polite offers and verbal thanks. It was plain that these young people, who had practically declared war, meant the hostilities to be conducted with the most rigid etiquette. The first meal in the music room of the *Maori* was really a model of decorum. When it was over, Drury said, as he arose from the table:

"You have done your duty very cleverly. I may say that, perhaps, without embarrassing you by an unwelcome compliment."

"It is not necessary to say anything," Margery answered, shortly. "My duty is sufficient for me."

Chapter VII.
MARGERY IMPROVES.

BREAKFAST over, Drury went on a tour of inspection through the ship, and found that there was an immense quantity of water in the vessel. He marked its height in many places in order to ascertain, as time went by, whether it had leaked in or had been merely shipped. This knowledge might be important later. A very high tide might float the *Maori* out again from the lagoon, just as she had floated into it. It would, therefore, be very important to know whether she was seaworthy. The time might come when it would be necessary to decide, at a moment's notice, whether to risk going to sea in the ship or to remain on an uninhabited island far from any of the great ocean highways. Meantime, there was much to be done. He did not spare himself.

The first thing was to provision and furnish the island, lest the ship might desert them on it. Drury worked all day at this. Miss Bute assisted, at her own request.

"I want to earn my own living," she said, somewhat peevishly, when Drury protested. Her nerves were still the worse of the drug. The situation was not well calculated to calm them.

"Don't you think you can do so aboard? You managed the breakfast so much better than I could have done, that it will certainly be a mistake if you oblige me to take up your work in order that you may have time to take up mine," Drury persisted.

"That will not be necessary. I can do a little of both. I—I—do not want to have any leisure. I should certainly feel—I mean I want to be occupied all the time. I do not wish to have time to think. What are we going to do first?" The determined voice in which Margery put this question settled the dispute. No one could refuse work to an applicant so earnest.

"I think I—I mean we—had better move as much of the tinned provisions ashore as possible. The other things will spoil immediately in this climate. They were only taken out of the refrigerating room as required, and, of course, that room does not refrigerate now when the engines are stopped. Besides, I have no doubt it is full of water and everything in it soaking in the bilge. We must make the best of a bad job before it is too late. A single day lost might mean very serious inconvenience later on. The provisions are our first necessity. There will be as much food lying about as will last us for years without going to the main stores. Arms and ammunition are the next to get out, and I am sure we shall find plenty on board. So now, since you are determined to help, let us get to work before the sun becomes too strong."

"I shall be ready in a few minutes," Margery agreed, and retired. In a short time she returned, dressed in her cycling costume. Drury, who had promised to wait for her before commencing work, regarded this metamorphosis with displeasure. He was very advanced in his opinions on politics, and finance, and sociology, as we know, and also on the woman question in general, but not in this particular. He liked advanced women; liked to talk with them, discuss with them, even debate with them, but somehow he did not, he found, want Margery to be an advanced woman. This was very inconsistent. It was explained by the fact that he was not thinking about her costume, but about the remarks the second-class passengers would have made concerning it. And these criticisms, he knew, would not be pretty, notwithstanding a certain correct but basic physiology underlying them. Then he remembered, with a jerk, that there were no second-class passengers about, and that consequently her costume did not matter; that, indeed, it was quite correct.

"It isn't done to shock you," the girl said, deprecatingly, "but I can't climb up and down that ladder every day, and forty times a day, in my frock." (The gangways had been carried away at sea). "I shall be more comfortable in this—I mean these."

"You could not be more properly dressed," Drury said, and the subject was dropped.

They worked very industriously for several hours, their first business being to construct a proper raft in lieu of the log which had already served as such. This raft, by a simple running gear of rope and pulleys, could be moved to and fro between the ship's side and the little toy creek which formed their landing stage. It was clumsily constructed, but it served its purpose fairly well. Before moving the supplies, it was necessary to prepare a place for their reception. This was easy, owing to the discovery of a small cave, which prehistoric tides had bored into the face of the solid rock, but which was now far above high-water mark. Here their packages and parcels would be safe from rain or blast, and here, without more ado, they commenced storing tinned foods of all kinds, and also rugs, wraps, cushions, rockets, a few flags, arms and ammunition (sporting rifles and the like, left by the passengers), fishing tackle, firewood, and everything that might come in useful. But long before this was done, the mid-day sun spoke out and bid them rest.

Margery, who had "knocked off" an hour before, managed the lunch as admirably as the breakfast. The table was even decorated with a bunch of purple passion flowers and some scarlet hibiscus blossoms, which she had gathered on one of her many journeys to the island. She was doing all that was possible to make the best of the situation, however mystified she still could not help feeling, as to its real explanation. She would have been glad to believe Drury's whole story. But parts of it surely strained facts too far. If she could have withdrawn some of the harshest words she had used, she would have done so willingly. But how to do that without agreeing to all the rest was more than she could plan.

In the afternoon Drury did another spell of work, and Margery kept to the ship, where she found plenty to do. When evening fell they were both tired out. Notwithstanding her sense of fatigue after her day's work, Margery made a special effort in the preparation of dinner. She got one of the galley fires lighted, after severely burning her fingers many times, and actually succeeded in cooking a small joint and a fowl. And they were not so badly cooked either, if allowance be made for the cook's inexperience of galley arrangements—no doubt admirable for those who are acquainted with them. The main thing was that it was a real dinner; no make-believe of bread, fruits, cold meat, and so on, but a good English dinner. And there was beer for one of the tired workers. The other abstained. After dinner they sauntered about the ship, the open warfare of the morning having already been replaced by what could not be called more than an armed neutrality. Passing the engine room in their aimless walk, Margery said, with a shudder, as she looked down at the great forest of steel:

"It is the most depressing thing of all, to think of all that—that—dead machinery!"

"Yes, it is dead enough," Drury said, in a low voice. The girl's description was not inapt. "The metal is there all right, but the metallic soul is gone. It is only the corpse of an engine-room we are looking at."

"Then it affects you as it does me?" Margery asked, with interest. Their voices were subdued, as though they stood by a deathbed.

"Oh, I don't know," Drury replied, absently. "I was not thinking about it so much as—" He paused and peered down.

"As—?"

"As the humans, the stokers, who used to work down there, when all those coal mines were open, and all those thirty-five furnaces were ablaze, and the heat even on deck was unbearable, and the only wind was a following breeze."

"Ah! It is too terrible," Margery said, with a little groan. She placed her hand unconsciously on his arm in the emotion of the thought. In a moment she removed it suddenly and turned away.

So far, the day had not been without its interests; but the evening was rather trying. It was not easy to go back on a subject which had already been discussed with such undesirable results, and it was not easy to ignore it. Margery's conduct had been so exemplary all day that she deserved to be forgiven for her incredulity in the morning, and its rather blunt expression. And the utter want of precedent which surrounded their position warranted a little deviation from the lines of conduct which might be judicious under ordinary circumstances. But even if Drury were willing to risk being accused of falsehood again, there was something about the girl which he could not quite understand. He was conscious that the distance between them, in spite of their common anxieties, was rather more than that of first and second-class passengers on the *Maori,* even if that distinction had not been permanently abolished. He made no special effort to bridge this distance. It was only fair that Margery herself, having been so completely mystified, should, in her turn, become a little mysterious.

For want of a better subject, Drury at last described a simple plan he had thought of in the morning for catching fish fresh from the sea. In the border of yellow sand which fringed the head of the lagoon, which he had passed in his first journey of exploration, there was a little depression, covering, say, a rood, which was noticeably below the level of high water. This he proposed to connect with the tideway by a slight channel which he could dig in an hour. Some fish, at least, would swim in when the water rose. It would be his business to see that they did not swim out when it fell. He was becoming quite eloquent when Margery interrupted, with a little shudder:

"I am afraid I could hardly manage live fish. Horrid, slimy things! You will have to kill them for me."

"Oh yes, of course, I meant that. And I'll—anyhow you must see the fish trap to-morrow," he added, hastily. "It will be some sport catching these piebald beauties. Seems a shame to eat them. Perhaps we'd better keep the pond full. It would be an amusement to watch them at close range."

Then the subject which had been in his mind all day could be delayed no longer. He attacked it with some hesitation, and the greatest delicacy. It was really very difficult—very unconventional.

"I am very sorry for you," he began; "I mean I recognise how hard it must all be for you—and— and—" He stopped short, and then said abruptly, "I recommend you to take stateroom No. 73, the port of which looks towards the open sea instead of to the bare wall of rock against which the ship rests. Your own stateroom, you know, is on the island side. Besides, 73 is at the end of a corridor I shall occupy 69. It is near enough to be within call. The island, as I told you, appears to be uninhabited. But if any natives should turn up, their first business will be to ransack the ship. They may come at any time, and if so, they must pass my way before they come yours. I shall bring your luggage up for you."

"I thank you. My luggage can remain where it is, and I can get what I require without troubling you."

"Very well. You know that I am here if you need me," Drury said, drawing a cigar from his case with the intention of lighting it, when Miss Bute left the room.

Now this very simple action had a strange effect on the girl. Overcome, as she had been, by the extraordinary events which, after various stages of confusion and horror, had arrived at a point where the last semblance of probability vanished, she would have been less moved by the announcement that all that had happened since she first awoke from her drugged sleep in the ladies' cabin of the *Maori* was only a myth; that the whole story was a dream. But there was a certain *vraisemblance* about this triviality that struck home. She nearly broke down. So he had sat the whole evening without smoking lest he should annoy her!

"I did not know you smoked. How was I to know you smoked—or, rather, I did not think about it. I am very sorry I forgot."

"It is of no consequence—none whatever."

She stood hesitating for a moment at the door of the cabin. Then she said timidly:

"Good-night !"

He arose and was about to offer his hand. But he changed his intention as to this, and answered quietly:

"Good-night."

Chapter VIII.
THE UNCHARTED ISLAND.

THE next day was one of very laborious work, for new business was on hand. Drury, who had always been rather observant, watched everything with the microscopic exactness of a man at bay—of one, too, who had another life as well as his own to guard. He found that the water in the ship had not receded perceptibly in the twenty-four hours for which he had marked it. This water, then, had all been shipped. It had not leaked in, or it would have gradually leaked out again, for it was now far higher than the comparatively shallow water in which the *Maori* lay when the tide was out. That was a great addition to his knowledge. He acted upon it as soon as he was certain of the accuracy of his opinion.

Many schemes for getting rid of the shipped water were considered, only to be rejected. To attempt to pump it out would be absurd, for three reasons. One, sufficient in itself, was, that the pumps were all choked; the second, that singlehanded he could not work them, even if they had been clear; and the third, that the pumper might work, if his health lasted, till well on in middle life, if not old age, before he could empty an ocean liner half full of water. It was in the second afternoon upon the island that his great thought came to Drury, and he acted upon it without further deliberation. He had seen the fire drill too often, not to know where the hose was stored. This he dragged up on deck, making many journeys in the process. He was worn out when he had finished his preparations, and, dinner being ready, he postponed his experiment until after he had dined. Miss Margery had not been idle either. She had again lighted the galley fire, and the dinner, which was laid on the little table in the music room, would have been creditable to the menage of any quiet family. Fresh flowers were on the table. Everything was as bright and cheerful as the circumstances permitted. The meal was very agreeable to the hard-worked youth after his severe labour. He ate heartily, and this time ventured to thank his hostess—or his cook—with sincerity, if with the same studied reserve which was now accepted by both as the special form of etiquette which must be observed between them. The thanks were accepted as frigidly as they had been apparently offered.

After dinner, Miss Bute played some pieces on the fine piano carried by the *Maori*. It had been a fine piano, but the drench of the breakers had sadly damaged it. Still, the few notes which sounded out of tune now and then, and the few others which did not sound at all, either in tune or out of it, while marring the execution of the piece from a strictly musical standpoint, hardly lessened Drury's great relief. It was exquisite to him to lean back on a comfortable seat and listen to any "noise." The dead silence of the ship was becoming dreadfully oppressive to him. It was not less oppressive to the pianist. She played on for nearly an hour, and easily discovered, as she played, the weak points of the piano, if not its strong ones, which were, in truth, altogether undiscoverable. The weak points she skilfully avoided, and made the most of those which were less weak. Before the recital was over, the performer was able to produce a sequence of sounds nearly as pleasing to her listener, and not much more meaningless, than the highest class music is to an ignorant audience. The first performance was thus a success.

"Would you care," Drury asked diffidently, when the music was finished, "just to pass the time, to see an experiment I am about to try?"

"Yes," the musician answered wearily, "I would like to see any experiment that would make this long day shorter."

"Come along, then." When they came on deck he showed her a piece of hose, the end of which passed down into the hold. He had previously cut the hose into lengths, tied up one end of one of these and filled it with water. There was plenty of that about. This length of hose, being air-tight, did not empty itself into the ship, but remained firm and full of water. Drury threw the loose end overboard. He had calculated the height exactly; the end of the hose hung within a foot of the water outside. Climbing over the rail and down by the rope ladder, he dropped, as it seemed, right into the sea; but he had the raft there. With a sharp knife—which has been mentioned before—he cut the end of the hose, and a fine cataract of water began to pour out of the ship; the hose pipe acted as a perfect syphon. The experiment repaid the trouble it had cost. It was repeated on a larger scale later on, and before a week had passed a good deal of water was got out of the ship.

When the experimenter swung himself back over the rail, there was a touch of jubilation in his voice, and his eyes were bright.

"Fine, isn't it?" he cried, as he leaped on deck.

"It seems to be quite successful, but what is the object of it?"

"Why, to get the water out of the ship, of course. And now that the experiment has been so successful, I think we are entitled to a little amusement. Let's go for a row."

"On what? The log or the raft?"

"Neither! You remember the little pair-oar your father was bringing out—at least it is labelled with his name?"

"Oh yes, I remember it. He bought it as a model for the colonial builders. It is by the best man in England—Clincher of Cambridge."

"So I thought from its lines. Well, we shall have to get that up. I have rigged a pulley, which will make it easy to get the little shell launched, and then I will row you to my fish pond—I mean, to where I shall make the fish pond. Indeed, it only wants a few yards of sand shovelled out, and it will make itself."

They got the little cockle-shell boat launched very easily, and clambered down into it. One of the boxes of goods, shipped by a hardware firm, which Drury had broken open more from curiosity than necessity, was fortunately filled with spades. He took one and laid it in the bow of the boat. Margery shipped the rudder with the smartness of one well used to the English rivers, and made fast the tiller ropes. The oars were dipped, and away the boat shot over the blue water of the lagoon. It was one thing to see the coral groves and the little fishes dart hither and thither, and bigger fishes splash, and the crabs scuttle, and the anemones fish for their prey in the comparatively shoal water where the *Maori* was stranded; but it was quite another, and a vastly more moving spectacle, to watch these wonders of the sea from the little boat, which passed over the deepest part of the lagoon, and to gaze, with undimmed vision, down through the crystal water, twenty fathoms deep, and see, not clusters only, but great shoals of gorgeous fish, flit like flocks of brilliant birds, among the coral trees, from grove to grove.

The boat's keel grated on the strand. Drury leaped out to assist Margery to land, with dry feet of and only an infinitesimal sacrifice of her spirit of independence. Then he showed her the long, low-lying bed which he had marked for his artificial lake, and the little tongue of sand, which, he declared, he could dig through in ten minutes.

The sun was setting as the digging was finished—all but the last yard, which the rising tide itself would sweep away, once the water began to pour over it and into the ready-made channel. As they waited for the tide to rise, Drury smoked a cigar, its fragrance was very pleasant—homelike. Margery approved it, but she did not speak. Her silence was not altogether misunderstood.

They had to wait longer than they expected, and the moon was rising before the water broke in. It was a splendid sight, as it poured in a phosphorescent cascade into the channel, and spread in a great blaze over the low-lying sand. It rushed hither and thither, reaching out long, ghostly arms of light, and pointing spectral fingers afar, where little natural furrows allowed it to extend. It plunged in burning masses into the deeper pools, and flashed into flamboyant breakers where the backward sweep met the onward rush. The moon climbed up, and up, and there they stood, spell-bound, and entranced by the beauty of the little picture. Then the water rested. The slide faded from the screen. The lights went out. The picture was off. The moon, herself, was dimmed by a handsbreadth of cloud.

Margery turned to her companion, and said, in a voice that was almost awed:

"It is time to go home"—the inadvertent word seemed to choke her—"I mean, to go back. it was very beautiful, but it is over now and growing dark. You might not find your way easily if the moon does not appear again."

"Oh, I'll find the way very easily. But it is time to be moving. We'll come back some day soon, and fish here with more success than the anglers on the Thames."

As the girl stepped into the boat, a cool breeze moved over the water. She shivered, although it was more the sudden change from the great heat of the day rather than any perceptible degree of cold which caused the sensation. Drury threw his jacket over her shoulders as she passed, saying carelessly:

"You might carry that for me, as I shall be rowing?" Margery did not put the jacket off, but she looked undecided for a moment. Then she tied the two sleeves loosely together across her breast, and replied:

"Very well; I will carry it for you."

The boat slipped into the water, and in another moment its bow was pointed for the *Maori*, a long, black line against the bank of rock on which she rested.

As Drury rowed leisurely "home," Margery sat silently in the stern, steering the boat automatically. Her thoughts slipped from conscious keeping. So, quite without knowing it, she commenced to croon over, rather than sing, scraps from the songs she knew, dabbling her slender white fingers in the tepid water over which the boat passed. Drury rowed carefully. His neatly-feathered oars hardly splashed as they dug up jets of phosphorescent fire from the sea. Margery crooned on, quite oblivious of the wrapt attention of the rower. She rambled from song to song—a line here, a snatch there. Sometimes the words were strangely inappropriate—marble halls, and the like, being a negligible quantity in that Pacific Sea. Then a phrase would come in quite fortuitously, but with quaint application:

"Row, row, under the stars."

At last the girl stopped the chance snatches and began one song at the opening line:

"Oh, Genevieve, I'd give the world
To live again the lovely past!"

And Drury winced when he heard the curiously significant verse:

"And such the trust that still were mine,
Though stormy winds sweep o`er the brine,
Or though the tempest's fiery breath
Rouse me from slumber to wreck and death."

The soft voice was very plaintive. The wail of the words lost nothing of their pathos from the way they were sighed rather than sung; nor from the strange scene of their singing, overhung with a purple sky, into which the tropic stars were rushing, constellation after constellation, by myriads.

"For heaven's sake don't stop!" Drury pleaded, when Margery ceased suddenly, and with a little gasp. "It is really delightful." He had not been rowing for some minutes, but the girl did not notice it till the great pulse of the Pacific moved the still water of the lagoon, and caused its placid bosom to swell in a long, slow answering heave, over which the "Star of Asia" rose easily, and then fell gently down, as a whole district of water sank beneath it. This arrested Margery's wandering fancy. The recall was something of a shock. She did not speak for a minute. Her eyes were wet. Without the slightest reference to Drury's exclamation, she asked:

"Why are you so anxious to get the water out of the ship? Is it worth the trouble? What difference does it make, so long as we can get everything we want?"

"Oh, it makes a lot of difference. For one thing, it might stagnate inside and be disagreeable. There will be some of it left in any case, but the less the better; and for another, the ship will be more sea-worthy without it, if she should happen to go for a voyage on her own account."

"You have spoken about that before, but, of course, we should not go to sea in the ship. We shall wait here, now that we are here, until we are picked up by a passing vessel."

"I—am—not—sure—of—that." He pulled a stroke between every word. "It might not be wise to remain."

"Why not? Better that than the madness of going to sea in—what do you call it?—a derelict ship."

"It might not!"

"Go on. Tell me what you mean?"

"This island is not marked in the Captain's chart."

"How do you know?"

"Because I have examined the Captain's chart, and there is absolutely nothing on it within hundreds of miles of where he last marked our position, which he did, as nearly as he could guess it, just before ordering out the boats. He could not, of course, on such a night, take an observation; but he worked a sort of dead reckoning from the place where he was last able to get a glimpse of the sun, and as this point was marked with a cross, dated, timed. and labelled, '*Maori* abandoned here,' I am certain that he gave the position of the ship, as nearly as he could, just before he quitted it, in the hope, I suppose, that if any vessel picked up the *Maori*, and boarded her before she sank, a look-out would be kept for the boats. It was a forlorn hope, no doubt; but a good captain leaves nothing to chance."

"I wish he had not left me to it—I mean, us," Margery corrected, hastily. This was her first tacit admission, since their last night at sea, that she believed Drury's extraordinary story. He was thankful for that, and pretended not to notice the slip and its correction, which he certainly perceived. He went on:

"So the Captain could not have known anything about this island. If he had, he probably would not have abandoned the vessel at the time he did."

"And all this signifies?"

"Oh, many things!"

"Of which the most important is?"

"Well, if you must know—-it signifies that ships do not pass this island."

They were at the *Maori's* side now, and the boat was drifting at her painter. Another moment, and they were on deck.

"Merely because it is not on the Captain's chart?" Margery asked, as if there had been no interruption to their conversation.

"Not at all. If it were on his chart, it would be on every chart. If any ship ever passed it, it would soon be on every chart, but—" He stopped a second, and, turning away his face, said in a low voice:

"It is an uncharted island!"

Chapter IX.
CONFINED TO BARRACKS.

SOME days passed away, not altogether unpleasantly, for there was plenty of work. When the island was well provisioned, and furnished with all manner of comforts, there were still undamaged stores to be moved up from the lower deck, where, although the water was well down, everything was still in a state of slop, and nearly everything in the form of food quite spoiled. The arms and ammunition, too, must be kept in good order, lest a native trading party might arrive in canoes, from any point in the compass, to barter for merchandise with war clubs or poisoned arrows. The breaking open of the few doors which were still locked, and the keys for which were not forthcoming, proved in itself an agreeable recreation, and was pursued with zeal. They gave themselves over heartily to the pastime. It was a grand distraction. And long excursions were made on the island. The explorers surveyed its length and breadth. They exhausted it. Then, when the life was beginning to prove monotonous, a great discovery was made—the specie room of the *Maori*.

It was not so easy to break into this; but unlimited patience knows no law, and these amateur burglars managed their business successfully, if with a clumsiness of detail which would have horrified the least expert professional. The boxes of gold were very strong, and well screwed up. But that only added to the fun of breaking them, when they resisted too long the pleasing process of unscrewing. The sight of the yellow metal had a curious effect upon the burglars for a few moments. They had never seen so much money before; not even in a bank.

"How much do you think it amounts to?" Margery asked, as earnestly as if there was a market round the corner for the money. Drury was delighted by her childlike eagerness. It meant much to him. It meant that her health was now fully restored; that she might, therefore, stand the strain of their great loneliness; might live till rescued. In spite of the serious misunderstanding by which they began their life on the island, and in spite of the instinctive barrier which he felt in a vague, subconscious way was between them, he knew that if anything happened to her—he could not, even to himself, put a stronger word on it; he could not say "fell ill;" he dare not say "died"—if anything happened to either, God help the other! So he was glad to hear her laugh brightly at her own earnestness.

"I daresay a hundred thousand." This indifferently, as if the sum was a trifle.

"A hundred thousand pounds! What an enormous sum!"

"Oh, it's nothing to what these ships sometimes carry," Drury answered, noting with pleasure the heightened colour on her cheek.

"But," said the girl, on a sudden thought; "what is the good of it to us in a place like this? We might throw it over the side and be nothing the poorer."

"What you say is perfectly sound at present, from an economic point of view," Drury admitted. He pursued the subject for a moment in an abstracted way, partly because he was not thinking very keenly about it, and partly from the pernicious instinct of instructing the uninformed which he had acquired from living too long in a little clique in which he himself was the most learned authority. Also it would be good for her if her interest were maintained.

"Yes," he went on, "if the value of a sovereign in a man's pocket is simply measured by the want of it in his neighbour's, we should be very wealthy if we could induce a large indigent community to settle here. But as the indigent community, if it came, would probably relieve us of the money the moment it arrived, and kill us in addition, perhaps we are just as well off by ourselves. Sort of splendid paupers! Aren't we?"

"Just what I thought," Margery agreed. "Shall we throw it overboard," she asked, slyly; "to prevent accidents?" His remarks struck her as rather transcendental.

"Oh, no—by no means! We'll chance the arrival of the indigent community, in the hope of one day making better use of the cash. But we ourselves must get away from this room without delay. It is enough to make us misers before our time."

On the same evening, when Drury had gone to inspect his fish-pond, Margery sat on a deck-chair under the awning they had rigged, and thought out a problem which was seldom absent from her mind. She had a book in her lap, but she had not opened it. Her cheek rested on her hand. Her attitude was very listless, suggestive of acute mental depression. She did not change her position for a long time, but sat quite still. At length she became restless and moved uneasily. The book fell on the deck.

She kicked it aside impatiently. Suddenly she sprang to her feet, and said aloud:

"I just believe every single word he said!"

That this did not refer to the last conversation between them will be gathered from her next soliloquy:

"Oh, I do hope that the boats got to some port, and that my father is safe."

This was followed by a more cheerful reflection:

"He is very much better looking than I thought at first, now that he is so nicely browned by the sun. Dark men like him look so well in these white suits. He is such a fine, tall, muscular fellow. And he is—he really is rather nice."

Just as Margery said this, she heard Drury clambering up the rope ladder. He jumped lightly on deck, and found her reading a cookery book, upside down, both as to the page and the covers.

"I was thinking, while I was away," Drury began by way of gossip, as he drew another deck-chair close to Margery's and lit a cigar —he had not now to ask permission— "I was thinking about a girl I used to know—"

"I am sure you miss her," Margery put in demurely.

"I—oh, I did not mean that. I was about to say that she was the only girl I ever met who had your splendid hair—hair exactly like yours."

"They say mine's red."

"Do they, indeed?"

"But it is, you know—a little."

"Then the other girl's must have been red—a little. It never struck me that way, however. It always struck me as magnificent. But what have you been doing all evening? Been lonely?" Which signified that he was willing to drop the heroic reserve if she approved. But it seemed that she did not wholly approve. Still, she answered very pleasantly:

"Oh, no, not at all. I have been reading. It's a valuable book to one interested in cooking. You could not read it, of course."

"Not that way, at all events. Is it Chinese?" Drury said this without malice, as he glanced at the book and its position. But Margery was rather put out, and she let him know it, too. She had a hasty temper, but not a bad one. Her retort, which was rather sharply worded for the occasion, was allowed to pass. The person to whom it was addressed was beginning to understand her better. He never forgot, either, that the most patient sympathy was surely owing to a girl situated as she was. On her part, the girl was fully conscious of his sympathy and grateful for it—so grateful, that before she left the deck she brought herself to mention the charge of falsehood she had made against him on the first morning on the island. It was an awkward subject, but she knew that she must withdraw the charge now that she believed it to be false. It took some time, however, to bring the matter round.

A soft evening breeze usually came in from the sea as the sun went down. The smoke from Drury's cigar drifted on it, in tiny blue wreaths. A long, low moan told that the distant bar was complaining as usual. Gulls and other fishing fowl began to circle about. Unseen wings whirred and whistled in the fast falling darkness. Across the lagoon, flashes of phosphorescent light marked the plunge of a Cape pigeon. Margery tried to speak—commenced—stopped short—began again.

"I'm sorry I doubted you that morning. You—you who have done so much for me—so much more than any other man in the world would have done. Forgive me!"

"I believe I have forgiven you," Drury answered in a serious voice. "I thought it rather hard at the time, but I did not make enough allowance for what you had undergone. It was certainly no ordinary experience to go to sleep in a crowded steamer, and awake next morning in this wilderness."

"But I awoke the night before."

"Yes, but you were only half conscious, and could not fully realize what had happened. And now let us say no more about it. I am glad, all the same, that you have mentioned it."

"And so am I," Margery said to herself as she left the deck.

Drury sat late on deck that night, and smoked many cigars. They cost nothing. He was well content. The *amende* was a slight one, but it was better than none.

Thus the little desert-island drama ran until circumstances altered so that a sudden change in the programme became necessary. On the fifteenth day upon the island, Drury came back from a fishing expedition with a startled face. He made light of his adventure, and maintained, in a chaffing tone, that he had seen a ghost— a real savage man's ghost. But the raillery in his voice was rather poorly affected, and Margery saw, with concern, that something serious must have occurred. He had always behaved himself so bravely, it was no trifle which put him out so. He positively would not tell, however, what had happened, even when Margery complained that it was unkind to keep her in suspense.

Next morning, Drury, as he passed hastily over the side, looked back to see if his going were noticed, or thought worth noticing. Margery was watching his movements, it is true, but there was too much of that hateful expression of "duty" on her face to please him. The confidence between them, which her apology established, was to be only momentary. It seemed to have practically passed away. He lifted his cap in a cold salute, and climbed down the rope-ladder without a word.

"Don't forget," Margery called after him, "lunch at one."

"If I am not back, do not wait for me."

"If you are not back, I shall be——"

"What?"

"Disappointed?"

"Duty?"

"Precisely!"

If he had seen the hot flush on her cheek, or heard the angry stamp of her foot on the deck, he would have gone away in better heart. Drury was not back for lunch. And he ate very little at dinner. His manner was still strangely preoccupied. Often he tried to rouse himself, and assume a cheerfulness he certainly did not feel. But the pretence was so poor, albeit made in all sincerity, that it did not impose on the lady of the ship.

"You have eaten nothing," she said at length. "You are ill!"

"No, no—not at all! I am only a little vexed. But it is nothing; it will pass very soon."

"Perhaps you will tell me what you see when you are away which upsets you so much, considering that I am at least equally interested with yourself in this island, and all that happens on it," Margery persisted. She was getting very anxious, and indeed, alarmed.

"Of course you are; but this is different. It does not affect you. It—there isn't any 'it.' I did not say there was. If I did, it was by inadvertence. And I want you to promise me something," he said, suddenly and earnestly. "I once spoke of 'compelling' you to do as I wished or ordered, but then I was beside myself. We understand each other better now."

He waited a moment, so she answered carelessly:

"Yes—no doubt!"

"Now, I want you to promise me that you will not leave the ship without my knowledge for some time to come, and that you will not leave it at all when—when the tide is coming in."

"Which arouses my curiosity!"

"A curiosity which, for your own sake, must not be gratified."

"How do you put it—a command or a request?"

"A request if you please; a command if you don't please." The words may seem rough, as here written. They did not sound rough to Margery. There was too much sincere solicitude, in the voice which uttered them, to pass the observation of a quick-witted girl. So she answered a little distantly, perhaps, but without the least temper:

"Then I am for the future, especially at the rising of the tide—"

"Confined to barracks. It really must be so." For about a week Drury behaved very strangely. Always at the rising of the tide, or when the last tide was in the night, early in the next morning he went away from the ship. On the first of these journeys he carried a long parcel, wrapped up in a piece of rough sacking. Once or twice, when this swung against the ship's side, there was a muffled ring as of metal clashing. In previous journeys of exploration, he had always armed himself with a couple of revolvers or a rifle, but on this occasion the long sackcloth parcel was his only accoutrement—to get it over the side without notice seemed to be his only care.

Margery noticed very quickly that the man's whole nature was changing for the worse, as the weary days of this miserable week went by. His resolute air, if at times a little masterful to be altogether agreeable, melted away. He was moody, even morose. He paid no attention. He never noticed the little changes she was making in the music-room. Pretty trifles were arranged here and there. Every day it was becoming more like a drawing-room, and less like an empty hall. How he lived she hardly knew, for he seemed to eat nothing. It was, she soon found, impossible to coax his appetite. Her dainties, prepared with such earnest care, did not tempt him. Perhaps he despised her cooking (which was really excellent). She taxed him roundly, and almost tearfully, with this one evening, when he declined point-blank to look at her bill of fare.

"Please don't trouble. It's no fault of yours; everything is perfect. But I can't eat," he answered, a little shortly, as he reached for a decanter.

"You don't require any pressing to drink I notice," Margery said, quietly.

Drury started, and the colour came for a moment to his face, which had grown very thin and haggard in the last few days.

Margery continued firmly: "I know I have blamed you in error, and I deeply regret it. At the same time, it's not quite pleasant in—in—the curious position we are, to find that you are beginning to drink to excess, which you know you have done every evening since—since this new fad of yours—"

"Since this new horror came into my day's work," Drury corrected, and the next moment was sorry that he had spoken.

"I wish you would tell me what the horror is?" Margery went on, with a touch of entreaty in her voice. "It can't be worse than to see you—to see you—changing every day. Surely you might stop this suspense. It is unbearable. And I won't bear it any longer."

At that, Drury arose and went over to where Margery was standing. She had left the table in disgust. He did not walk very steadily. His eyes were bloodshot. He smelled abominably of spirits. Altogether he was not looking very attractive at the moment.

Margery, with a white cheek, watched this drunken man tramping unsteadily toward her. He brushed against the table twice, broke a few plates, and used some words with which we have no concern, as Mr. Barrie puts it. Then he filled up the cup of his transgressions, and put his arm round her waist. She disengaged herself furiously from his clasp, and, snatching up a knife from the table, stood at bay.

The effect of this dramatic action on Drury was sudden and extreme. His condition was really more owing to his previously abstemious habits than to any present excessive drinking; added to which, the evident distress of the new business he had on hand had certainly accentuated the effect of any liquor he had taken. His sudden metamorphosis was a surprise to himself, as well as to the girl, who stood with a heaving bosom, her eyes dilated, her white fingers firmly clutched round the handle of a knife. He was sober almost in a minute. He waited for another before he spoke. When he did so, his voice was calm and almost without a trace of emotion. He guarded it very carefully.

"You are mistaken—not for the first time, either, if you care to recollect," he said, with deliberation. "But it does not matter. I have suffered so much in these past few days that I really wanted some human sympathy, which I was absurd enough to expect from you. I grant that I have been clumsy. I will repair my error. I have just thought of a way to rid you of my disagreeable company. I have some work to do, which may occupy me a few days yet on this island. That work is partly in your interest, and partly otherwise. When that is finished, I shall take the pair-oar and row over to another island I discovered yesterday, only five miles away to the south. We did not see it in the haze, the only time we looked that way, about a week ago. You can have this one and the ship, and do what you please with everything. You won't be subject, then, to the inconvenience of having to defend yourself— with a knife." His voice broke, and he stopped.

"If you could contrive to be a little more intelligible," Margery put in, slipping the knife back on the table rather shamefacedly; "it would be a mercy."

"If I am unintelligible, it is in your interest," Drury answered, simply. "You would probably thank me, if you knew the cause." So far, he had been fairly rational, but he now spoke stupidly and foolishly. He was altogether ridiculous, and knew that he was so.

"When I get my business here finished, I shall start for the south island, and find out if it is inhabited, and, if it isn't, I can return for supplies once a month or so—"

He was interrupted. Margery really could not help it. She thought she was nearer tears than laughter; but she was mistaken. It was hysterical laughter which had overtaken her, and this is resistless. Her face was turned away, but her shoulders shook. She was either sobbing or laughing. She could pretend no longer; the laughter would not be restrained.

"I am glad," Drury said, grimly, "that my suggestion amuses you."

"Oh no, no! I really can't help it. It's nervousness, and nothing else. I am really trying not to laugh. It's what you said about—about—coming once a month for supplies."

"It's very funny, I dare say. But I don't see the point of it."

"The point is, that I don't think—that is—that a month is a very long time," Margery said, steadily. She had got the hysterical fit under control.

Drury looked with a puzzled air at the now serious face opposite to him, and then burst into a good-humoured laugh. "I see it now. You are quite right; I have been talking rubbish. There! Will you shake hands upon it?"

"Yes; but you must tell me now what your business at the coast is."

"To-morrow I may tell you."

"To-morrow you must tell me, or I shall find out for myself."

"Don't say that. I have your word of honour. I may be able to release you to-morrow."

"To-morrow!" Margery said to herself, as she commenced clearing away the remains of the unsuccessful dinner. "I almost wish I had not seen to-day. But to-morrow!" Her shoulders went up in a little reckless shrug as she added:

"To-morrow I will 'break my arrest.'"

Chapter X.
THE HARBOUR BAR WAS MOANING.

NEXT morning, as the tide came in, Drury said "Good-morning" quietly, and left the ship. Margery returned his salute with a careless nod, making believe to be very busy about some routine matter which absorbed all her interest. She did not wish him to suspect her purpose. He went away, consequently, without the least idea that she had made up her mind to follow him.

When Drury had disappeared round an angle of the cliff, Margery scrambled down the rope ladder with a dexterity which practice had made easy to her. She was a practical athlete by this time. Her hands and face were as brown as a berry—brown, not red—notwithstanding her complexion, which, unfortunately for its possessor, mostly goes peony with the sun. But Margery had the proper shade of tan, and knew it. Otherwise she would have carried her parasol more regularly. No doubt she owed her smart "style" in clambering up and down ropes (in her cycling suit) to Drury's instruction, but she was a painstaking pupil, and owed it to her own patience that, in a few weeks, she had gained the agility and grace of a trapeze performer. But, indeed, her movements had been always graceful. The raft was floating, of course, close to the beach where Drury had left it, but, by pulling on the tackle which moved it to and fro, the girl brought it to the side of the ship, and in a minute she was on dry land. Her emotions were not very agreeable, acting, as she was, in a measure, the part of a spy.

"But he has no right to keep it from me. It may be some new danger that is threatening. It must be something dreadful, from the way he has changed; he's not a bit nice now. I hate to see him drinking as he is doing; he's getting horrid—not that I mind—at least, not that way. Still, when one must live on a deserted ship, with only one companion, the conduct of one's neighbour becomes a serious matter. Anyhow, I shall find out what it all means to-day. The reality cannot be much worse than the miserable suspense."

Miss Margery's last sentence may be a fairly reliable generality, but in this instance it did not hold; for the reality proved very much worse than the suspense. She walked cautiously along the strip of yellow sand which fringed the great cliff on the north shore of the lagoon, about half a mile from where the *Maori* lay. Keeping close in to the rocks, and peeping round every boulder before she passed it, she saw that her way was clear before she showed herself. There was no sign of Drury anywhere; he had completely disappeared. The in-blowing breeze brought with it the dreary dirge of the waves breaking on the bar. This gave the girl an unpleasant thrill.

"Ah, that dreadful sound!" she cried. "One cannot shut one's ears to that. Night and day it never ceases. That harbour bar is always moaning." But for a little while thereafter she forgot her clandestine purpose. The morning was glorious; the scene very beautiful; and the ozone blowing in from the ocean—it was grand. It was difficult, under the circumstances, to remain altogether depressed; to remember only the disagreeable limitations of life. Her fine physical health would not be denied. Her spirits rose in spite of her own instinctive feeling that it was wrong to be elated when he who had faced almost certain death for her, who had practically thrown away his life for her, was in such poor condition, whether his troubles were real or only imagined. It was like laughing in church, or being gay at a funeral. It was hardly respectable; but she could not help it. Little snatches of song came warbling to her lips, to be repressed with difficulty. The glorious blue of the sky; the deep blue of the water; the yellow sand; the tinted coral; the green of the trees on the southern shore, with their great festoons of giant parasites; the breath of the sea and the breath of the flowers—it was hard to be altogether insensible to these!

When she was near the entrance to the lagoon, Margery's high spirits sank suddenly, and soon died away. She walked steadily on, talking to herself in a low, serious voice: "I am afraid I am getting nervous, just as I am coming near the end. But I must be brave; he must not see that I am afraid. I do not have to drink to keep my courage up. Pah! I am beginning to despise him—poor boy, I do so wonder what is troubling him!" She rounded the entrance to the lagoon. The open sea was before her. "What can have come over him? Yes, there he is! I thought I should find him soon. Whatever is he doing? I'll keep behind this rock and watch."

Drury, his jacket thrown on the beach, and his shirt sleeves rolled up to the elbows, was digging in the sand just above high-water mark—a very innocent pursuit for a man who pretended to such important business.

"Can he be losing his reason?" the girl gasped, turning very white. "Then I shall be imprisoned here with a lunatic!"

Margery's cry was not altogether without cause. Drury's actions were really extraordinary. He jumped up out of the hole which he had been digging, and in which he had been muttering to himself and jabbering like an imbecile. When he stood beside the bank of sand he had thrown up, he leaned upon his spade, and said aloud:

"Cast your dead men upon the waters and they will return again after many days." He laughed suddenly, and continued:

"Curse them! that's the worst of it. I wish they would stay in the waters where I put them. But they must come fooling back to demand the right of burial, which is a job I have no stomach for. Suppose I must do it, for her sake, otherwise she'd find the whole business out."

"That's what she is going to do," Margery commented, in a whisper

Drury laughed again in a loud and unconvincing guffaw. He was either demented, or laughing to keep his courage up. There was certainly no mirth in his laughter. He looked down into the hole he had dug, and commenced to sing in a weird, droning voice:

> "Nigh to a grave that was newly made
> Leaned a sexton old on his earthworn spade?"

"He's not old, but he's beginning to feel that way," he said wearily. He looked at his hands, which were badly blistered by the unusual work, wiped the perspiration from his face, and stretched his arms as though fatigued. Then he sang again:

> "And these words came from his lips so thin,
> I gather them in—I gather them in."

Drury stopped singing, threw down his spade, and stood a moment irresolute. Then he went to his jacket, and took a flask from a pocket in it. Resolution had evidently failed this deal. He appeared, so far as the now thoroughly frightened girl could see, to drink a good deal before he put the flask back into the pocket. He threw the jacket again on the ground. Then he took a boat-hook, and walked a score of yards towards the sea. The tide had already fallen, and there was a long, bare reach of sand. When he stopped, Margery could see a bundle lying close to the water, which she had not noticed before, so intently had she been watching the lunatic who dug holes in the sand for a pastime. Drury reached out the boat-hook, and fastened it in the bundle, standing as far off from it as possible. He then turned back towards the hole he had dug, dragging the bundle after him.

"Gracious heaven! It is a man he is dragging. He has killed him, and will bury him before my eyes!" Margery ran from the shelter of the rock which hid her, and called out in terror:

"That is a man you are dragging in that brutal way!"

"It is," Drury answered, thickly—he was half-dazed with the drink he had taken—"a dead man. Go away; you should not have come here. I ordered you not to leave the ship." He went on angrily; "Go back at once; this isn't a woman's business."

"Have you killed him?" Margery cried, without noticing the command.

"Not I!" This sullenly.

"Are you sure, then, that he's dead?"

"Been dead three weeks."

Margery had to rest her hand on the rock beside which she stood to steady herself. Her knees shook. She would have fallen but for this support. Drury's speech was very coarse, but he must have suffered much; and his condition at the moment, if not very creditable to him, must to some extent palliate, if not excuse, the bluntness of his words.

"Who is he? Who—was it?"

Margery could hardly speak, but a desperate fear which had suddenly gripped her demanded relief—the relief of instant contradiction, or the knowledge of the worst. The agony in the girl's voice struck the gravedigger, although he was in no mood for troubling himself about trifles. He was about to speak, when he paused, swayed unsteadily on his feet; then recovered; dragged on the boat-hook. Without answering the question, or indeed speaking, he threw the body into the hole he had dug, and commenced to shovel in the sand.

"For pity's sake, answer me if you can!" She walked a few paces toward the lonely grave, and cried out in anguish, "Is it—is it any of—of—them?"

"Sullivan, third officer of the *Maori*."

So the boats had found a beach, if not a port, on which to discharge their crews. This was the end of all—all dead! Her father dead! The stricken girl gasped once or twice hoarsely before she could speak. With a hard effort she contrived to say:

"Have—have they all come in?"

"Most of them. I buried your—him—on the island. The rest I shove under the sand as they come in. I have neither time nor strength for more—No, you don't! Don't faint there, for I could not assist you now. I dare not come near you, after what I have done this morning, until I have changed my clothes. Get away from here, for heaven's sake—and don't go that way. Keep the upper path by the open sea. Keep as far as possible to windward of my cemetery!"

Margery Bute went slowly back to the stranded ship. She hardly knew where she was going, nor what she was doing; and it was purely automatically, and without conscious intention, that, as she paced slowly by the shore, she moaned to herself the music of our great Dead March, keeping time thereto with her footsteps. The whole gamut of human sorrow is covered by that awful music. The heart of man cannot conceive a bereavement which it is inadequate to express; an emotion of loss which it cannot convey. Margery cried and wailed to herself, all through its massive cadences, its magnificent misery. A double orphan now, without a near relative alive, it was impossible for her to resist the despair which over-whelmed her. She gave in, as it were, with a bad grace. For indeed she tried valiantly not to give in; but the burthen was too heavy.

Sometimes she stopped mechanically to watch the waves come in, and then resumed her walk, unaware that she had paused. One great billow diverted, for a few moments, her attention from her own thoughts. She watched it almost with interest as it marched majestically shoreward, a splendid line of green water. The land breeze touched its crest, and a hundred tossing plumes streamed in the air. As the water shoaled, the wave lost weight, but gained in height and speed. It rushed onward now, taller, more slender, less stable with every yard which was added to its race. The green brightened to a lighter green, until the girl could see the sunlight right through the emerald ribbon. Then pausing a moment as though uncertain—it lifted up its voice, and burst with a roar into a cataract of snow. From the seething mass, long sheets of foam shot out over the hissing sand, covering it with a frothing garment. Then the water swept back, leaving innumerable little rivulets to follow, these cutting their own channels in the sand. By a solitary piece of rock, that was splitting up, there was a harsh growl of seaworn pebbles.

When the wave had returned to the waters whence it came, Margery once more resumed her funeral march. A hundred yards further she halted suddenly.

"Oh, God forgive me! And I have never even given him a thought. And he is out there—out there—working for me. My poor boy! My poor boy!" she wailed. Then she cried fiercely, and her eyes flashed as she spoke; and her bosom heaved with quick breaths. "Poor boy, forsooth! He is a splendid man. And I—I cannot even let him know that I—that I—like him." After a long pause, "No, it would never do," she said softly; "I must not let him know."

Now this unselfish thought of Margery's for the man who was "working" for her was not without its own reward. For it blotted out for a few merciful minutes that hideous scene upon the sands, and for the same brief space it hushed the melancholy music of the bar.

But the years were many and the years were long before she was able to look back with only a peaceful regret on that Harbour Bar and its moaning.

Chapter XI.
A Night of Terror.

DRURY'S absence was longer than usual that day. He did not come for lunch, which was a pity, for a dainty little meal had been prepared. Scarlet hibiscus, purple passion flowers, and many other tropical glories were in the room or on the table. The music-room of the *Maori* was scented with the breath of blossoms and foliage, with just the faintest odour of delicate cookery. For Margery had done her very best, well knowing that her comrade's appetite would need much tempting on this day. Although she had acted so far very loyally to him in the commissariat department as a matter of duty, this day she knew how well her best efforts had been deserved. Her own misery was not allowed to interfere. She could indulge that later. But he did not come, and she gazed sadly at her masterpiece, until it was apparent that she must give up hope. Then, without eating a single morsel, she removed the untouched meal, and threw herself on a couch, with her handkerchief to her eyes. "Will he never come?" she sobbed. It was a weary day for her.

It was late in the evening when Drury returned to the ship. The girl heard his coming with intense relief. She was thankful to see that his face had no trace of the morning's orgie. He had stayed away until he could present himself decently, and was, in consequence, late for dinner as he had been late for lunch. This, indeed, did not trouble him. Margery begged to be allowed to get him something to eat, but he declared he could not swallow food. He could only smoke, and he did so zealously. When his cigar was lighted (Margery struck a match and held it for him), he leant back in his chair and was silent. She did not speak for a long time either. Neither cared to allude to the scene upon the sands that morning; and the little gossiping topics which had gradually grown into their lives, chief of which was the always present speculation as to the chance of a stray ship drifting their way—how best they would attract the attention of the vessel; how signal her, and so on—these were too trivial. Small talk would be a sacrilege. Drury found the silence growing more and more embarrassing, for he feared every minute that in the next the girl would question him more closely than he cared to answer. So to put aside the distressing subject by raising a side issue, he said:

"I am sorry for the shock you had this morning—"

"You have had many such shocks, and made no complaint."

"What I wished to say was," he continued, without noticing the interruption, "that—that—if you feel too nervous to-night to go to your own berth (she was already dreading the coming darkness), I will make one of these chairs as comfortable as I can for you, and—if you wish me to remain, we can pull through one night without sleep. We shouldn't—either of us, I suppose—get much rest in any case."

"It is very good of you," Margery said gratefully, for she would have given the ship, the island, all the Pacific Archipelagos for this alternative. But as she spoke, she looked up at him, and saw his tired-out white face, and so she went on bravely, with a hardly perceptible break in her sentence: "but it is not necessary. I am not at all afraid."

"Very well. Then I think I'll turn in, for I am really tired out; but—I shall not—I mean I always sleep just as I am now, to be ready for any danger, and if you call, I shall be with you in a moment." He could say no more to encourage her, so he left the cabin.

Margery had a book ready. She brought the lamp from the table, and set it on one of the wicker-work arms of her chair. Then she deliberately set herself to read the night away, for she knew that in it there would be no sleep for her. Time passed very slowly withal, and the lazy hours were terribly long in passing. She looked at her watch every five minutes, and then, by a great effort, resolutely refrained from looking for a long interval, in order to see what a great stride Time had taken, when again the watch would tell how far he had travelled. Six minutes only had passed, so the plan was not a great success. She then placed the watch on a table beside the book, and recommenced her now double task of watching the printed page with one eye, as it were, and the hands of the watch with the other. The night dragged on. The scene on the sands acted and reacted itself, in spite of every effort to force it out of mind. The murmur of the waves hummed in her ears. Before her eyes the broad flakes of milky froth floated like giant water lilies on the shallow, shore-coming remnant of the breakers. The sudden flash of a hundred swooping wings, as the sea-birds dashed past, startled her by their wonderful reality, though they were now reproduced in a brain-picture. And at last, as was inevitable, into this mental cinematographe there drifted the figure of a man—a man dragging something with a boat-hook over the sand. It would have been a relief to scream as this picture came upon the cloth, but she clenched her white teeth firmly; the time for screaming was not yet. Her nervousness increased every minute, until she was hardly rational. Weird shapes began to take form in the twilight of the room, lit by the single lamp. Imaginative fancies rose up, swore that they were facts. Dreadful thoughts were driven into her brain by every tick of her watch, which kept on remorselessly muttering and hammering, until a fantastic atmosphere was created, into which any ghoulish thing might creep. This atmosphere was hard to breathe and live in sanely. But Margery would not flinch; she would not give in. She would face the ordeal until its end. It was her turn of duty; she would remain at her post.

At last the girl's nerves began to give way altogether. She now heard what she thought were real sounds and voices, which, when she sprang to her feet, seemed suddenly to be stilled, only to begin again their dreary growling when she resumed her seat, and once more pressed her hands over her ears. Once, after starting up, the sound she thought she heard appeared to continue. It came from without; from a great distance. She could not tell whether she really heard it, or only imagined she had, as before. She opened one of the ports and listened. There was no doubt now; the sound was real enough. It was the wild song which the harbour bar always sang when the sea was rising, or when the flowing tide came in. It was too dreadful; its associations were too immediate. She closed the port and resumed her reading, or rather began again to gaze at the open book—and the watch beside it. She read resolutely. It was not an interesting book either; it was a novel, naturally, and on any sensible plane of existence it might have passed an hour away. But it was not sufficiently distracting for a nervous girl, on a deserted ship, whose only living companion was a half-demented man, who had spent his morning in burying rotting corpses on the seashore, and who had, from the nature of his occupation, been driven well over the thin border line which separates normal intellect from sheer hysteria.

Another hour dragged its slow length away, and then there was another sound which broke the ghastly silence of the music-room. It was as weird, as wild as the voice of the bar—and it was as real, too. This was more terrible; for this was *within* the ship!

It came from the hold. Could there have been stowaways? A foolish thought, for they would surely have made their presence known sooner. And this was not the sound of a human voice, this that was moaning far down in that lonely ship. It was altogether too sepulchral for any living thing to utter. Margery stood up unsteadily and grasped the lamp, saying valiantly:

"I will make sure before I awake him. I will not—I will not disturb him for a nervous fancy. He has had enough to bear."

She passed out of the cabin and crossed the saloon, proceeding in the direction from which the sound appeared to come. All was quiet now. Her heart almost stood still. For a minute she thought she could hear its feeble beating; then that was drowned in another sound—a great groan that swelled up from the hold. Taking her courage, as the phrase runs, in both hands, Margery Bute went to the head of the companion leading to the lower deck, and in a voice which she hardly knew to be her own, called:

"Who is there?"

Another groan wheezed up from beneath.

"Who is there?"

For the second time she challenged.

Dead silence! The girl actually did hear her heart beat now as she waited. Then again strange voices began to mutter and grumble far beneath, and the groanings became at last a sort of chorus to which she could no longer listen and keep her reason. For the last time she cried aloud:

"Who is there?"

Then the mumbling, moaning terror took articulate voice, and to the distraught girl it spoke. And her answer to that message was a shriek, which rang through the ship fore and aft.

"Good heavens! what has happened?" Drury cried, dashing from his stateroom in time to catch the flying figure as it rushed distraught, with no consciousness of its purpose or the direction of its flight. Margery clung to him with both arms, like a frightened child, and cried and laughed by turns, growing rapidly and very evidently exhausted. Soothing and caressing did nothing to allay her terror. He must speak firmly to her. It was hard to do so, but he could not allow her dangerous excitement to continue.

"You must stop this instantly," he commanded. She moaned, and shivered, and clung to him.

"What has alarmed you?"

"I cannot—dare not tell you. I am going mad, I think. Don't drive me further."

"No, but I'll drive you back to your senses, though it distracts me to be rough with you. Drop this nonsense, and let me get you some wine."

"Don't leave me alone, for mercy's sake!" Again the girl clung to him.

"I certainly will not leave you. Come with me."

They passed into the music-room together. There was no wine there. Margery had removed it early in the day for reasons that then seemed sufficient to her.

"We must go below," Drury said, with some disappointment. "Come along!"

"Below! You must not go below!" she cried, with a half-suppressed shriek.

"If you will only be sensible for three minutes, and allow me—"

"You must not go below!"

"Why not? What on earth has come over you?"

"Oh, please don't go below! There's something awful. You must not go on my account." She caught his hand and held it tightly in both her own.

"By God! I'll search this ship from stem to stern on your account, and find what has terrorised you. I was a coward, this morning, when you discovered me burying the man—the last man, I hope. I admit it, and I'm not ashamed of it, for I've had to do more than most men. But I'm not a coward now—not when you are near me, when I may have to fight something living for you. The dead men are rather beyond me; but this thing is alive. Let me go; loose my hand!" But she clung piteously to him, and he could not thrust her from him by force.

"It isn't anything natural."

"Natural or supernatural, I am not afraid of it. I am going to find out what it is. I'd face the devil for you!" After the poor figure he had recently shewn, he was desperate now to prove himself a man of courage to her.

"I cannot let you go! I will not let you go, George, stay with me, and I will tell you."

Notwithstanding the tumult of his emotions, he did not fail to notice that, in her distress, she had called him by his Christian name for the first time. He was glad of it; but, of course, he set no store by it. The girl had simply spoken out in her terror. He would not make capital of it; he would only remember it as long as he lived.

"Tell me," he said, very gently. The modulation of his voice would really have soothed a frightened child.

"It's a voice!" she gasped, stroking and petting his hand, with dumb appeal.

"I don't care if it were ten thousand voices."

From the depths of the ship the long, low groan came wheezing up again. It was a strange sound to hear in that always silent ship. For a moment of time the man's courage well-nigh failed, and but for the presence of the girl he would have flinched. But instinctively he moved between her and the direction from which the sound was coming, and then, hardening his heart, he said quietly:

"You must let me go now. I shall be back presently and tell you what it is, and—"

"No, no! You must not go!" Margery cried, and, clutching him in terror, she hid her face upon his shoulder.

"It is the voice—his voice—Sullivan, third officer!"

Chapter XII.
THE FLOWING TIDE COMES IN.

NEXT morning it was Drury's business to prepare breakfast. Margery was still too weak, from the effects of her fright overnight, to do more than superintend. She gave her moral support, however, and would have derived a little benefit, in the form of mild amusement, from the clumsy efforts of her assistant, only she was too downhearted. Eventually, the meal was not such an utter failure as it would inevitably have been, had the cook been left to his own culinary resources.

Daylight having now been some hours on, and darkness being, in consequence, comparatively forgotten, Margery was easily persuaded that the weird groans which had disturbed her the night before were not supernatural, but simply the result of the straining of the ship, which the tides were beginning to force out of the bed that she, by her own weight, had made for herself in the sand. But the girl was really very much the worse of the nervous strain, and Drury noticed, with alarm, that the effect of the shock did not pass away as quickly as he had hoped. As the day wore on, Margery's listlessness or lassitude plainly increased, in spite of the strong effort she made to appear in her usual health. The pretence was too evident. It broke down at last, when the daylight died and the hateful darkness was reborn. They were sitting on deck, watching the last of the light, when the girl began:

"I am very sorry I—I—" Brave as she was, her voice choked into a rather miserable little whimper. "I am afraid I—I don't like to go to my cabin—"

"Why should you, if you don't wish it? We'll sit on deck. It is much cooler and pleasanter up here. It's quite a happy thought." He was already bustling about looking for wraps for her, lest the wind might change during the night. When it blew right into the lagoon, the night air was cool, if not cold.

"Now, I must talk to you," Drury said, cheerily, when he had made her comfortable. "You are downhearted and nervous, and I must try to keep you amused, and prevent you from moping." He knew nothing, and cared less, about the social chivalries of a drawing-room; but he knew much, and cared still more, about the easily-guaged responsibilities of a man to a woman in distress and danger. All the real chivalry in his nature was afire. He must fight faithfully for her now, or never more stand at ease in his own self-respect.

"I am afraid I shall tire you," Margery replied. "I want you to talk to me to-night as you have promised—of course, not mere chaff, although that is pleasant enough, when one has a mind for it. I want you to talk in the way I overheard you one evening after we left San Francisco—Oh, I wasn't eavesdropping—I wasn't indeed. You had a little crowd round you, and I thought you were making a speech; and I certainly thought you spoke very well."

"I remember the evening, and I was making a sort of speech. There was a Californian on board, and whenever conversation ran short, he used to draw me on with one or other of my favourite subjects. It was only when I was pumped out that he would own up and admit the joke. He was a curious man that. I am sure we never had two ideas—not half an idea—in common, and yet I felt very sorry for him. He certainly did his best at the very last for me—but I didn't mean to speak of that. What a beautiful night it is! Don't you enjoy the breeze?"

There was a faint stir in the air, the first breath, as it were of a coming breeze. Slight as it was, it was a pleasant change from the stagnant atmosphere which had lain on the ship all day. As the short night passed, this little stir in the air gathered strength, and before morning a delightful wind was sweeping in from the open, and the murmur of the bar, which had gradually swelled into a loud lament, became an angry roar.

"You spoke of your favourite subjects?" Margery said. "What are they? It is rather odd, but we have been so busy and so—oh, just so busy—that I hardly know you a bit better than when we first met. Oh, dear no, that is not what I meant at all!" she corrected with a rush. "Of course, I know you now to be the—the—"

"Thank you. But don't say any more; you would be certain to get the length of an anticlimax. Your artistic reticence is much more effective," Drury interrupted, with a pleasant laugh.

"What I mean is," Margery began again with determination; "everything has been so strange, so unbelievable, and we've been so taken up with this island and the chances of getting off it, that we've hardly ever spoken of an ordinary topic—say, such as that of your 'favourite subjects.' What are they? How delightful!"

The last exclamation referred to the breeze, which just then seemed to take another great breath, and, lifted by it, the lagoon spake with a solemn voice. Away on the coral rocks, far over the shingly lands, that long sigh told where the tired heave of ocean had found rest. Instinctively the man moved his chair closer to the woman's. He drew hers closer to his own in a protecting way that was not resented. They did not speak for some moments. Then the woman broke the silence, with a little cry:

"What a dreadfully dreary sound that was! It is so desperately lonely! I never felt the mere loneliness so much before. If it were not for you, I should go mad. Say something, for heaven's sake—anything to keep our thoughts away from this terrible place. What was it I asked you? Oh, yes—your favourite subjects! Bravo! Make a speech."

"You'll work yourself into as hysterical a state as you were in last night," Drury said, seriously but gently. Then he went on quickly, talking against time (he had done so before in the same cause). "My favourite subjects! Oh, they are very many I could not even index them at a moment's notice. I believe principally, I think, in human progress. I consider a first-class ocean steamship a grander wonder of the world than the biggest pyramid in Egypt: the one is only a monument of brute force and slavery, the other is a triumph of brains and free labour. I believe that the present asinine method of paying a man, not for what he *does*, but for what he *has*, will find early death and suitable burial. I believe that a man will, towards the last day, be paid as much for doing work which is vitally necessary for society—probably hard, and possibly disgusting—as he is now for writing a book, or painting a picture, or chipping out a statue, all these, primarily, for his own gratification. Of course, I know that brain-work is said to be the hardest, but I think there'll be trouble when every man wants the hard work, the brain-work—and the brain pay. I believe that overwork and underwork will alike be abolished when humanity is humanised, and that war will be ended when it is generally known to be ridiculous as well as wrong. And I believe that, in its own good time, sense will cover the land and common sense the people."

He rhymed all this out in a sing-song voice, that came near to intoning. It filled the purpose for which it was intended. It interested Margery. The Uncharted Island was forgotten for the moment. That was well. It would return to memory soon enough.

"But you would not abandon Art?" she asked, eagerly. "You would not separate life from everything that was beautiful in it?"

"By no means. I only wish that so much which is ugly could be removed from it; that all the absolutely needless misery and suffering could be eliminated; that a little more justice and fairness could be imparted into it." He was not talking against time any longer. He was talking because he must. He had got on a favourite subject in earnest. He left his chair and strode to and fro on deck. He forgot the island and all its unchartedness.

"What is your theory," Margery asked, in a soothing voice—for the excitement had passed over to the other side—"of the destruction of all the civilizations which have preceded ours?" She put in this question to quiet him. She thought it would create a diversion, and that he would prose over it with comfortable conventionality. It failed in its purpose very completely.

"The extinct civilisations all perished," he answered sharply; "because they were admittedly or practically founded upon slavery. That was bad for the slaves, and bad for the slave-owners. Perhaps you have read Lubbock's books on ants, or heard Dallinger lecture?"

"Yes, yes. But you think our civilisation will be permanent, final?"

"I do. I think it will be wise in time."

"Listen to me," Drury hurried on, with animation. "You don't understand my point of view, because you know you were 'born a little conservative;' but you are a clever girl, and I think you will surely grasp this:—In an ideal society, the class which, in the commonweal, digs into the bowels of the earth; dives into the depths of the sea; tunnels the mountain; bridges the river; mans the lifeboat; drives the express; the class which goes half-clad that parasites may pore over fashion plates—half-starved that society may surfeit—to that class belongs the future. It shall have the spoils. The merchant and the middleman must go. The gamblers are going and will very soon be gone. Even the true captains of labour can no longer lead when every toiler will have education enough, knowledge enough to be his own captain; or collectively, they, among themselves, will have knowledge enough to be their own captains. And the pretty little tinkers, and the deft little solderers, the romancers, poets, painters, players; all the merely ornamental entities in civilized life, whose so-called work is play; all these will certainly be admired and applauded, but they really won't be paid. There is a phrase with which you must be familiar—'Art for Art's sake.' It is essentially an artificial and superficial phrase. But granting it all the wisdom which is attached to it by the low cerebral types amongst whom—perhaps I should say amongst which—it is popular, I can give you a better phrase, one which will displace it and succeed it—'humanity for the sake of human nature!'"

He paused, breathless. He had allowed himself to be carried away, and felt awkward and almost abashed at the strenuousness of his own words, once the heat of the moment was passed. Besides, the absurdity of the situation instantly thrust itself upon him. The futility of his language in such a scene was too evident, apart from its monstrous impropriety, considering its *raison d'etre*—the edification of a lonely girl, suffering from nervous strain. It was surely banal, if not entirely brutal. Margery was silent. She hardly understood the rhapsodical deliverance, and from what she did understand she partly dissented. Still she was glad of it. It really helped to distract her. She persisted:

"This human progress—what direction will it take?"

Drury looked at her serious face with an amused expression, and answered:

"Is thy servant a prophet?"

"No, I don't expect you to prophesy. Only, just what you think."

"Well, I think I may undertake to prophesy that the desire for personal appropriation, the double value which the sense of proprietorial right now lends it—the possession by oneself and the dispossession of one's neighbour—this will absolutely lapse. Physical courage being unnecessary, will be no longer desirable, and will probably be looked upon only as a mild form of ferocity. Sympathy will be broadened so as to include more than one's mere family, friends, or country; and as man becomes more an intellectual animal and less an emotional animal, the passions—anger, hatred, jealousy, even love itself—will be less intense than with us. Love will go last, because, while, of course, it is purely egoistic, it is the most altruistic."

"What a colourless world that will be!" Margery said, with a little sigh.

"Leaden-grey throughout—to you or to me. But it will suit the people famously who will live in it. A mosstrooper, if he could be resurrected, would die of civilisation in a week."

"Then you think that the millennium is at hand?"

"Not quite—if you count a few centuries as a reasonable interval."

"But you think it will come?"

"I think that man will surely, if slowly, work out his own salvation from his own suffering. And I think he has nearly suffered enough to deserve it. He will have earned it; and I hope he will think it worth the cost."

"Do you admit that woman has shared this suffering, and will help in the salvation?" Margery asked, mainly because she saw that he was interested. Much of what he had said was beyond her.

"Shared it! From the harem days down!" He threw out his arms with an unconscious gesture of despair. "Mother of God! would any millennium be worth all *that*?"

A groan sounded up from the depths of the ship. The tide was rising fast. The *Maori* was again complaining of her imprisonment. From the ocean without, the water was racing in with a foaming rush. The stars were paling, and the dreary cries of the early-rising sea-birds were beginning again. Everything was more weird, more dreary, and more unspeakably lonely than ever. Drury felt a little hand placed timidly in his. The clasp was rather hesitating, but the fact that it was given at all meant trust. He brushed his theories and his "subjects" from his brain, and said, hastily; "Let me tell you a little story. I intend publishing a very small edition of it, consisting of one signed copy, which I shall present to you."

"That will be a great compliment. And you are going to tell me the plot now—I mean the ending of it?"

Margery said this quickly, for she was glad to get him away from his wild talk.

"I am afraid," Drury answered lamely, "I have only got the introduction ready." In fact, he had not even that outlined; but he was a good story-teller, and he trusted to his imagination.

"Please tell me," Margery cried. "That will be famous!" It would be certainly much more interesting, she felt, than the sociological discourse, and even that had been better than nothing.

"I am commencing it like this," Drury said desperately, for indeed he began to doubt his own extempore powers, now that they were to be so immediately tested:—

"Two children are at play under the big trees on grassy dells they hide, and call to each other. They are alone. The material world has passed out of their lives. There is a long vista through the beeches. The eyes of clay note only a pretty stretch of shaded turf, stippled here and there with rustling points of yellow, as the dying leaves whisper together; and the fleshly ear hears only the deep sad sigh of the great overhanging branch, that moans for its lost offspring, withering to dust beneath its shade. But the children! What to them are the crude barriers of mere material sense? Hand-in-hand they steal gently on, noting much, wondering much, imagining so much more, that soon down that long avenue of verdant shadowland their twin souls sweep on wings of meditation—away into the paradise of the unknown, into the gardens of romance, where many valiant deeds are done, and feats of arms take place, and great castles frown, and gentle thoughts and pleasant courtesies mingle and blend, till the whole is a beautiful kaleidoscope of delight. See that weird gulf under the upturned roots of the fallen fir—a robber's cave! Observe the little dell where the sunlight flickers through a netting of twinkling thorn—my lady's bower! Then the broad open space where the deer are grazing! It is populous with warriors bold and with beauteous dames, for to-day there is a tourney in the land, and only the brave deserve the fair. And, out on the wide stretch of moor beyond the park, where the bees drink deep of heather sweets, 'St. George for Merry England' is the cry, while the Saxon spears clash loud with the claymores of the Scot. Thus the children pass onward, hand in hand, and prattle out their little thoughts and strange fancies.

"But now the clouds are lowering, and the sun hides himself, and the grove is dark and fearsome, and great drops of rain splash angrily through the leaves above, and the wind begins to moan a solemn dirge. Then these two very strange and curious children, who care not for toys or hobby horses, hardly even for wooden soldiers, hurry homeward, their little faces rather white, indeed, at all this atmospheric anger; but each one still half bold in the presence of the other. And a day comes quickly when a dark-draped woman holds one little restless pair of hands in hers, and bears one lad brave but mute companionship. For to speak at such a time were a shame—even to a child. And she helps him through; ay, till the little lad, to show how well he means to play the man, stands still and chokes down a sob, to spell out the simple line which tells the ended story of him who was as his very life—but who has now passed lonely through the dark valley. This memory will last him, the one who was left, through many years. It will be interred only with his bones."

"That's how I commence. Rather fine, isn't it?"

"It is too pathetic for me. Why do you begin so sadly?"

"Oh, I mean to work in the dead child's influence on the other's life. A sort of dual entity will be vested in the boy that lived. I think I shall make him have, as it were, two souls—his own and the other's. It will be an interesting psychological study."

Drury stopped abruptly. He was at the end of his matter. Then, whilst they waited in silence, a great change passed over the still starlit sky, and presently, in a shower of golden arrows shimmering over the distant sea, uprose the sun. In that garish light their faces were woefully wan and white. But they made little of it, and passed it off with a laugh, which, indeed, had not much sound of mirth. And just when Margery was wondering might she not—should she not—dare she—shew some little extra tenderness to this true friend of hers, the friend, who was looking anxiously at the surface of the water, suddenly left her and dashed over the rail. He was not long away, and when he returned he said, quietly but ominously:

"Last night the water reached a higher point than ever before—ever since this ship was stranded here!"

"That means?" She asked with a gasp.

"It may mean nothing. Or it may mean that we shall lose this ship, unless—"

"Unless?"

"Unless we are willing to go to sea in her."

Chapter XIII.
A Forlorn Hope.

"YES, it is quite possible. When the water rises to the point which I have noticed it must sometimes do, by the rocks about, it may tear the ship out of the sand. Then, as the tide ebbs, she may drift out with it," Drury said next day. He spoke in an easy manner, but there was a serious element in the matter of his remark which it would have been hard to disguise. This was not the first time the subject had been discussed by them. But it was the first time that it was discussed with any semblance of possibility, and this time the subject had a certain stinging actuality in it that produced a numbness in one of the parties to the debate.

"What will you do?" Margery asked quietly, but with an anxiety that was only too evident.

"I shall do what you wish."

"But I mean, do you think it wiser to go with her or remain? Answer me fairly. You have tried to guard me from much, and—I shall not thank you now—but you see I am not to be kept from the knowledge of the worst, even for my own good. How do you think the chances lie? Tell me the whole truth."

"I consider that it is quite possible this vessel, if she once got out of the lagoon, might float until she fell into the track of ships. It is also quite possible that she might sink in the first mile. But it is, so far as I can judge, useless to expect to be taken off this island by passing ships, since none pass. So we may live our lives out here in peace and plenty, with a little monotony thrown in. We may also sink or swim with the ship, if she floats out and we go with her."

"What do you advise? I trust your judgment, and I—I rely upon you. I have had sufficient reason for doing so." She looked him squarely in the face for a moment as she said this, in a low voice.

"I simply advise—what you wish?"

"I wish to sink or swim with the ship."

"I agree."

"Then we sink or swim together—" Margery choked over the words, stopped suddenly, and turned away. Drury did not appear to hear. At least, he made no sign of having heard. The girl instantly resumed her habitually distant manner. It may be called 'habitually distant,' but, as we have seen, it was intermittingly the other way. The intermittent intervals, however, were so brief they would not be worth counting.

The wind, which now came every day, was heavy with the strong breath of the great ocean over which it had passed. It crooned aloft in the tattered rigging of the *Maori*, and wailed over the breakers on the bar. And every day that it blew the tides rose higher, and the great ship strained to be free from her self-dug grave. Twice in the twenty-four hours the lagoon was swept by a racing current, which dashed in and out with the force of a tidal wave. The ever-strengthening song of the sea without rose higher, and now the harbour bar was always moaning.

For many days they feared to leave the ship except at low water. Their excursions on shore were very short, and they always returned from them hurriedly. Indeed, there was nothing in the little ocean islet to see that they had not seen a dozen times. So they watched the rising tides with undisguised eagerness, and both were willing to face the great risk of the sea. The unconventional life, notwithstanding its somewhat desperate drawbacks, had been a rather interesting picnic for a time, and the sea and the scenery were undeniably fine, the air invigorating, and the ship comfortable. But they tired of it. Perhaps it was because the island was too small, or too far away from the theatres. Anyhow, the desert-island life did not seem to suit them, in spite of the many resources of civilization contained in a well-found ocean steamer, which they had to help out the primitive glories of earth, and sea, and sky. Besides, the island itself had associations which they could hardly forget. Only one sad pilgrimage to the lonely grave by the sea was made. Drury refused permission to revisit it, fearing that the action of the waves might any day expose the bodies of the dead, and he knew the shock would be serious, if not dangerous, to the girl. And Margery herself was dropping into a habit of obeying him without protest, when the issue was of serious moment.

As the days went past and the tides raced ever higher, Margery Bute watched eagerly the waterway to the open sea. Through that gateway her imagination sped always on tireless wings. And Drury, too could not help a furtive glance now and then toward the blue beyond the bar. This did not prove him a lukewarm lover. It only proved that, as you cannot civilize the savage in a single generation, neither can you return the complex human product of centuries of civilization to primal conditions with any chance of success—inside the first few weeks.

Meantime, life on the island settled down into a little groove which ran as smoothly as the routine of a grand hotel. The ship's supplies were, of course, inexhaustible, so far as two persons were concerned, and they were not spared, if they were not wasted. As to the friendship between these two persons, it neither waxed nor waned. Margery, after her little display of anxiety for her companion in her night of terror, and the more friendly emotion which she had shewn on that which followed, relapsed into an indifference which sometimes seemed rather ungrateful. Drury could not help observing this. He was hurt, but he was too supersensitive to admit it. He did not wish to cheapen himself to too mean a figure, and he succeeded rather better than he thought.

Thus, when running down from the bridge one day, he slipped and fell to the deck, he was agreeably surprised by his reception. His forehead had struck the handrail in his descent, and he got thereby an ugly gash, which bled freely. He was obliged to look for Margery, to get him something to bind up his wound, and found her arranging flowers in the music-room. He had no idea that he presented so blood-stained an appearance, or he would not have gone to her. When she saw him she turned ghastly white and seemed about to faint. But in a moment she was rushing for towels and bandages and water; and a trained nurse could not have dressed his hurt better. It is probable, too, that a professional nurse would not have crooned so many cooing little motherly encouragements over her patient. He must keep perfectly quiet or the bleeding would not stop; he must not stir; she could ease the bandage, if too tight—tighten it, if too slack. She would make him a nice cup of soup, for she knew he was weaker than he pretended, and so on. And when Drury discovered that he was her "poor sick boy," as the cool, deft fingers tidied the bandage, he felt extremely glad that he had knocked his head against a handrail, and found himself speculating agreeably on the possibility of further similar misadventures. Next morning, when the invalid was too plainly convalescent, Margery appeared to have lost all interest in her "case."

They were climbing one of the little cliffs which rose rocky and bare of vegetation, northwards, on the day that Drury was discharged from hospital. As usual, they were talking about the desperate chances of escape which any day might bring to them. Far beyond the cliffs stretched the everlasting sea. A heavy swell was on, although there was little wind. The horizon was ribbed by the great waves. The immensity of the ocean was impressive;

indeed, rather depressing. They looked at it for some minutes without a word. Why should they speak when each knew so well what was in the other's mind? The *camaraderie* between them, if strictly limited, was at least sincere. It was a terrible venture. But they would not shrink.

"Besides, you've got to know so much about the ship," Margery began, without introduction or explanation—neither was required; "that, as I told you, I trust implicitly to your judgment."

"I fear I don't know very much about it, after all," Drury answered. "Of course I have worked up flag signalling and one or two other things which may be useful."

"I often wondered what you were doing with the flags," Margery put in, little thinking where her comment would land her. "So you were actually practising?"

"Yes; I wanted to be smart about it in case of emergency."

"Many a time I was dying to ask you what you were doing, only, you know, that then we weren't—then—"

Margery's pause was a very full stop, indeed.

"No, we weren't, at first, very good friends. But we are now; aren't we?" This question was asked shyly. The answer was a little irrelevant:

"So you can signal a passing ship in a way that they will understand?"

"Oh, yes, I can signal them all right." The tone in which this was said suggested that the question was a disappointing answer.

"But don't expect too much from my seamanship," Drury went on presently. "It will be what is called 'a masterly inactivity,' at best."

"I don't think so a bit," Margery put in confidently. "You have managed everything splendidly so far."

"Thank you. But to manage our ship single-handed at sea, I should require the ingenuity of that toiler of the sea who re-engined, lowered from the rocks on which she was impaled, and launched successfully and unaided a big steamer with—what was it he had? A penknife and a piece of string, I think! You know that sort of thing used to do very well in story books. But it's not practicable in real life. Indeed, it would not pass muster now even in story books—. Look there! See the flying fish!"

"Splendid—but the tide must be rising now," Margery said, anxiously.

"That means we must go back. We must not let the *Maori* leave us stranded here. That's an ugly place to get down; give me your hand. Oh, bother it! I can't be always standing on ceremony! I'll lift you down." He did so before she could prevent him—that is, if she wished to prevent him, which is more than her historian knows.

They climbed down the cliff again, and walked leisurely to the *Maori*, for the heat was oppressive once the wind from the sea was cut off by the mountain spur. When they got on board, a surprise was in store. The slight list of the vessel was corrected.

The *Maori* was resting on an even keel!

But this day passed and nothing unusual happened. They dare not think of the next tide, or what it might bring forth. It was too full of fate. At the rate of increase which they had observed, it would touch the highest water-mark on the rocks. If the *Maori* did not float upon it, she would lie in the lagoon until she rotted, and they would live on the Uncharted Island until they died.

The great moment came at last. A strong wind blew all day. When evening fell, the tide flowed in tumultuously. It seethed, and hissed, as it swept past the stranded vessel in swirling eddies, and rushed inland, a foaming current. It burst into phosphorescent fireworks as the darkness deepened. It splashed and gurgled and filled the lagoon so full of water, that many of the little landmarks, which they on board had come to know, and had even given names to, were submerged under the rushing tide. And it struggled and tugged at the *Maori*, wrenching her this way, that way, forcing her to its will, so that at last the ship was torn clear from her moorings, and when the tide ran out, she slipped out upon it.

At the very last moment there was a slight pause of indecision on board. The vessel was already afloat, drifting down the lagoon, but they could easily leave it by the raft which was towing after. Margery weakened a little at the great crisis, and said in a nervous way:

"It is not yet too late."

"No," Drury answered; "it is not yet too late."

"I have troubled you too much, I know. But just now, for the last time, say what you think is best."

"It is best for us to go."

"You are sure?"

"Yes. It is best, because you would die of despair on this island. If you have to die in the sea, it will be less protracted and altogether more desirable?"

"But you? Your wish?"

"I do not signify," he answered with a shrug.

"Then you do not really care?"

"For myself, I really do not care," Drury answered somewhat fiercely. No matter how it ended, it could only end badly for him. Failure meant the island for the term of his natural life, with a necessarily artificial companionship with this girl. Success meant the absolute loss of the girl, not immediate, perhaps, but permanent. Once they were sighted by a ship, it was "Good-bye, sweetheart." He could not, therefore, be very jubilant. But, of course, he could do his duty, and he meant to do it.

His passionate exclamation did not pass his companion's notice. That she fully appreciated the ring of despair in his voice he knew from the pain in her face as she looked quickly toward him. He did not mean to give her pain; he would have cheerfully, as he had boasted, fought anything natural or supernatural to save her from pain; more than that, and better than that, he would manfully have worked his fingers to the bone to save her from pain. And yet he had quite gratuitously pained her, and he had seen that she had suffered—-and he was glad of it. The war of sex is sometimes, even with the best, rather bitter. Happily, with the best, the bitterness is not always brutal.

She came up to him in sheer distress, and said, softly, as she put her hand on his shoulder with a caressing stroke, which turned his bitterness to joy unspeakable: "I hope you won't say anything like that to me again. It hurt me very much—no, no, I know you will not do it again. And now—now we are starting on a terrible voyage, and you know we have only each other to look to for sympathy, and—and I have been rather stiff with you, I know; but—but everything is so awful—"

The *Maori* drifted quickly on the rushing tide, which brought her into the centre of the lagoon, where the current was stronger. This was fortunate, for she would now, at least, have a chance of passing out through the narrow entrance without striking. The motion of the ship had a strongly exhilarating effect on her two passengers. They were braving much, it is true, but there was something inspiring in the feeling that the vessel was once more afloat. And why might she not continue afloat until picked up? Was she not as likely to stand a roving life on the ocean wave as any derelict that sails the seas? Thus they encouraged each other, as the helpless ship drifted, in the early morning, down the lagoon—past the little capes and bays they knew so well, past the belts of golden sand, and the high peaks where the seabirds built.

Then the crisis came, for the ship was now in the entrance where the cliffs closed in, and those on board almost held their breath as she grated harshly against the perpendicular rock on the north side; staggered back from the impact; struck again slightly, but without serious damage—then passed out clear. Over the bar she plunged, bow on, beam on, stern on. Big a ship as she was, the waves threw her about with alarming force, and dashed great showers of spray over the deck, so that the two passengers retreated to the upper bridge, their faces wet with the briny mist, and neither of them very sure of having acted wisely in this desperate venture.

At last, with a fragment of sail, which had blown loose on the foremast, drawing a little, the *Maori* went before the wind and put to sea.

Chapter XIV.
DERELICT.

THE *Maori's* progress was naturally very slow; and although she was favoured by a slight current in addition to the wind, it was late on the second day of this strange voyage before the Uncharted Island began to blur into a faint haze, far away in the blue distance. The two passengers watched it grow fainter and fainter, with a melancholy interest. It had been their home for a little while—secure, if lonely. And now that they had gone down to the sea in a helpless ship, who could tell what peril might arise in a moment? So they watched the island till, in the darkness of the coming night, it was blotted out of their sight, nevermore to re-appear.

Under her rag of a foresail, the *Maori* drifted day by day in a "slow but sure" manner, until she blundered into some stronger current—probably the South Equatorial or the Counter Equatorial current. Drury had no means of discovering his position, or, rather, no knowledge of the use of the instruments by which it might be ascertained. Then the vessel's speed was accelerated. It was now probable that she would float until she struck the track of ships, if no great storm arose. Her hull must still be sound, for she was not leaking perceptibly. The Captain of the ship watched the horizon every day through a glass, so long as the light lasted. Not a sail was seen. Margery was not downcast. She had already borne herself very bravely against misfortunes under which most girls would have broken down, and she was not going to lose heart now, when every day strengthened the chance of being picked up by a passing ship, and brought rescue a few miles nearer. Her spirits rose with every dawn. Her life on the *Maori* afloat was not altogether free from anxiety, and it was by no means idle. But it was delightful, after the hopelessness of life on the *Maori* ashore. There were, as before, the Commissariat duties to attend to. They were attended to with zeal. She knew the galley now as well as any cook knows his own kitchen. And she worked with a will. Her handsome face very often bore the traces of her devotion to pots and pans. She usually presented an excellent imitation of the stage "general," the smudge on whose nose only adds piquancy to an otherwise attractive appearance, without in any way lessening the ideality of the part. The pleasures of Hope are sweet. They were always whispering encouraging things to her. "To-morrow we may be picked up," she said to herself every evening. "We may be picked up before night," she said every morning, marvelling a little sometimes at the apathy of the Captain, who watched carefully for passing vessels, it is true, but who did not seem at all disappointed when none passed.

Drury, indeed, was daily becoming more and more afraid of being picked up. And he had a very rational foundation for his fear. He reasoned thus: the *Maori*, having proved quite seaworthy, would drift on the Equatorial current, or whatever current it may be, until she would probably beach herself harmlessly somewhere from whence she might be reported. So far as he knew— not being a seafaring man, his knowledge was not exact— if he could report the ship from anywhere, her salvage would be due to him. This would certainly be a splendid fortune for a man who had taken his passage with only forty-five pounds in his pocket, after paying for his ticket. He had a vague but correct idea that a passenger could not claim salvage unless he could prove that he was instrumental in saving the ship. But surely he could prove that. If he had not pumped out the *Maori*, she would still be hard and fast in Margery Bute Bay, as they had named the lagoon. Further, Sir William Bute's governorship was gone with the Governor, and this had been openly spoken of as the last resource of a broken fortune. Margery Bute would then be only a poor, perhaps a penniless, girl. He forgot that she might share the salvage, if the Company so decided.

During this voyage, Margery began very craftily indeed, but systematically, to lead the conversation at meals, or when they were walking on deck, after the nighlight was swung. She did not, perhaps, quite lead the conversation, but she contrived to edge it over to one side—that of society subjects, dogmas, and doctrines. Drury regarded these as the most complete and adequate presentation of twaddle with which he was acquainted, and he was very sorry to see a clever girl shew so much interest in what he considered dull nonsense. One evening the debate on the value of such knowledge waxed warm—Drury disputing its worth, and Margery maintaining its necessity—when the former suddenly stopped in the middle of a sentence. He turned to the girl, and, putting a hand on each of her shoulders, made her look him in the face.

"Oh—you—you artful girl," he said, with great solemnity.

"What do you mean?" Margery answered, boldly.

"You have, you know you have, been surreptitiously—trying to teach me etiquette!"

Margery blushed guiltily, and looked very much embarrassed. To put the subject aside, Drury said pleasantly, "Don't mind me, my dear little—my esteemed teacher. For if you could never make me a success as a society man—which you couldn't—-at least you have taught me to be less of a bear than I used to be."

"You were always extremely nice," Margery corrected, in a low voice. The lessons in deportment were discontinued.

It came at last.

"A sail! a sail!" Margery cried, as she ran forward to where Drury was preparing a lamp for the nigh-light.

"Where? In what direction?"

The lamp was dropped on deck and smashed to pieces. He rushed to the starboard rail on which the girl was leaning; her arm outstretched, her face expressing excitement.

"It isn't a sailing ship. It's a steamer!" she cried. "There it is!"

And there it was, hull down as yet, but from the direction of the smoke-line, which was beginning to show on the horizon, it was probable that the steamer would cross the *Maori's* bows within signalling distance.

"Oh, do hurry!" Margery implored. "Get the flags ready, so that no possible mischance may occur."

"I will get the flags at once," Drury said, coldly.

The distant steamer bore down rapidly on the *Maori*. Her hull was soon visible, then the white, foam bank against her bow. Her lines were unmistakable. She was an unarmoured cruiser, and her name, as they discovered later, was the *Orlando*. Drury made only one bid for the salvage of his ship. He spoke in all sincerity, for he did not know that the *Maori* had already been sighted by the look-out on the *Orlanlo*, or that the cruiser was bearing down to enquire what was the meaning of "stopped engines" on a large steamer in mid-ocean.

"We shan't need to feel under any oppressive sense of obligation to them for taking us off," he said, in an apparently absent manner.

"I think we should be grateful to them all our lives, and every day of our lives," Margery corrected, with enthusiasm. The excitement had brought a bright, but natural, colour to her face. Now that she was animated by the prospect of an early realisation of a hope so long deferred, she looked her very best—and that was very pretty, indeed.

"Oh, as to gratitude," Drury continued, in the same calm tone; "they will pay themselves handsomely for any trouble they take with us. The *Maori*, with her cargo and her specie and everything, ought to be worth half a million. That would be ours if we could contrive to drift unaided into any port. It will be theirs, or their Government's, for taking us off." As he spoke he made a signal ready for running up.

Margery leant upon the rail for a moment. So he wanted the ship for himself, and did not mind sacrificing her life, most likely, on the very off-chance he had mentioned. It was a terrible disappointment, for more reasons than one. She would probably have broken down now, only that she had become used to bearing up. But this was hard. Her dejected attitude betrayed her emotion very eloquently. The cruiser was evidently passing at some distance. She would steam by, and leave them once more on that dreary ocean. The flapping of the little flags, as Drury ran up his signal, startled her. She grasped the rail tightly, and asked, unsteadily:

"What have you signalled?"

"N.C. It's an international code flag-signal, and they'll understand what it means, no matter who they are."

"What does it mean?"

"In distress; want immediate assistance."

"Oh!" That was all Margery said, as she turned to watch the cruiser. But two big drops trembled on her eyelashes for a moment, and then smeared her face unbecomingly.

The *Orlando* stopped and lowered a boat, which was soon alongside. Drury let down the rope ladder, and when the officer from the cruiser came on board, stated briefly that he and the lady who was with him had been left, by oversight, when the ship was abandoned; that the vessel had floated better than was expected; and that he would now be obliged if he and his companion were taken off without delay. In return for which he, with much affected politeness and magnanimity—and a little bitterness which did not pass one listener unnoticed—begged to present the *Maori* (8,000 tons, general cargo, specie roughly estimated at £100,000, and so forth) as a trivial *douceur* for the trouble he so much regretted to impose. Their private luggage was already packed, and he begged the assistance of a couple of men to transfer it to the boat.

All this was puzzling to the officer from the *Orlando*, who looked, as well he might, rather mystified. If a page from the "Arabian Nights" had been, at a moment's notice, personified and included in his round of duty, he could not have been more surprised. But, of course, he did not express his astonishment just then. Instead, he ordered up the men required, and in half an hour they were all on board the *Orlando* (returning from a scientific expedition). In five minutes more every man on the cruiser, from the Captain on his bridge to the humblest stoker, declared that Miss Bute was the handsomest, the most accomplished, and the most lovable girl in the world. Some of the stokers, owing to professional duties, were obliged, as it were, to make their mark; that is, to vote on hearsay evidence; but they agreed in the general verdict without any difficulty on that head. The scientific people were less enthusiastic than the naval men. In a matter of this kind scientific people have no sense.

The voyage of the cruiser home was much longer than had been anticipated owing to the tow. To Margery, however, it was an intense relief. After the Uncharted Island, its normal monotony and supernormal horrors, it was a resurrection to life, and her spirits rose with it. But Drury found it a very unwelcome change. He had given up all hope of ever being more to Margery Bute than a trusted friend—he had surely earned that. But he felt instinctively, as he saw her surrounded every day by her little circle of admiring officers, that he was out-classed—that she was amongst her own "set," even if there were no ladies in it. And he could not disguise from himself the fact that Margery did not seem to feel the absence of the ladies very keenly. She managed to do without them cheerfully, aided and abetted of course by the officious officers. Drury sulked rather stupidly for the first week. Then he gave in with a good grace. He had been rather self-sufficient, it is true, but he had broadened mentally with his varying fortunes. He was now too big to whine. He had left self pity behind for good. It is a good thing to leave behind.

One day a little midshipman, who had been intensely interested in the romantic story, which was common property on the *Orlando*, spoke to his hero:

"She would rather have you than the whole jolly lot of us, and I, you know I—well, perhaps I shouldn't say it." The midshipmite was too much of a man to say more. Margery had certainly been particularly gracious to him, because she really liked him, and he might have boasted a little with some show of reason, only that he was not made that way.

Drury looked kindly at the youngster, and although he would not have discussed such a subject with any other on the ship, he said to him in a correctly patronising voice:

"She is grateful. I know she is; but that is different. You will know what I mean when you are older."

"Oh, I'm not such a baby as you think," the lad replied with spirit. "I know what I am talking about, and I know that after having behaved like a real downright hero and no end of a brick, you're just going to act like a big booby; that's all."

He clapped a glass under his arm and moved off with the dignity of a post captain. He was certainly hurt by Drury's cool reception of his wise advice, but far more stung by the reflection on his youth. That was quite unpardonable.

It was unfortunate that on the same evening an equally well-intentioned mistake was made. It might not, perhaps, have been a mistake on any other evening. Coming so soon after the earnest but indiscreet intermediation of the midshipman it was a fatal error. Drury was standing by the side and watching the foaming track of the *Orlando* listlessly. He had got away by himself from all the crowd of questioners, who were always willing to hear the strange story of the *Maori* rehashed, as a welcome relief from their own threadbare subjects of conversation.

"Ah, well," he said rather mournfully to himself, as he reflected on the midshipman's advice; "I am afraid she is only a sad little snob after all. She certainly misses no opportunity of showing me that she is grateful. But can't I see as plain as the sun in the sky that she is at home amongst these fellows? She never treated me as she treats them, except once or twice, and then she seemed to be sorry for it afterwards. They're always laughing and making her laugh. Shouldn't wonder if she has recollected by this time that I was only a second class passenger. Oh no, I shouldn't have said that; she's straight and true." A hand was laid on his arm. He thought it was the midshipman again, and said lightly, knowing that the boy had been vexed by his non-acceptance of well-meant advice:

"Come to make friends? I am sorry I offended you. You are a fine little chap, and I am much obliged for your good opinion, but you shouldn't"—

"You might take the trouble to look round when you are speaking to me."

It was Margery. She spoke in that demure manner which she could assume very naturally. Drury was nonplussed for a moment. Presently he recovered, and said with an unaffected laugh:

"Forgive me; I thought it was your midshipman."

"Oh, Harry! He's a nice boy. I like him, but I have come to scold you."

"Scold away, please."

"I shall divide my scolding into three heads," Margery said sententiously, stretching out the fingers of her left hand and proceeding to count the heads upon them.

"Firstly, you have been behaving very ill-naturedly to me since we came on board this ship, which mercifully has a crew, and likewise engines going, and everything."

"I thought it was the other way about," Drury interrupted. "But I'll plead guilty to save the time of the court."

"Secondly, why have you been behaving so?"

"Well, I really didn't think it mattered. There are such a lot of other fellows behaving the other way, you know. I didn't think you would miss me in the crowd."

There was a touch of bitterness in this which did not pass unnoticed.

"Seriously?"

"Seriously I think the sailor men will be waiting for you to sing to them. Do you want to have me court-martialled, or whatever they do with civilians by spending two whole minutes in my society? You don't think of the risks you are thoughtlessly running me into."

"I said, seriously."

"And now I say, seriously." He took her hand gently and, after hesitating for a moment, pressed it to his lips. "You belong there, among that sort of people, if not these particular persons. It is out of gratitude that you leave them and come to me. I appreciate your motive. It is creditable to you, but you must not think that I would make capital out of any trivial help I may have been to you—that you are under any obligation to me. You go back to the world as free as you left it—and your world is not my world." He spoke quietly, but with intense feeling. It was breaking his heart to give her up, but he would have her with her own free will or not at all.

Margery looked thoughtful for a moment, and then said suddenly:

"Very well; I shall go back to the sailor men. They are very pleasant; at least they will not order me away, as you have practically done."

"I—!" But she was gone, and it was too late. No subsequent opportunity was afforded him of repairing his error of judgment. His offence was severely punished. He accepted the situation without complaint. In any event the voyage would not last forever, and the moment it was over all was over! This reflection, however, did not afford him all the consolation he endeavoured to extract from it.

The long absence of news of the *Orlando* had occasioned some official uneasiness before the cruiser was reported from Valparaiso. This was the nearest port where she could make land with the *Maori* in tow, and the towing process had been tedious. It was impossible to get up steam on the derelict, owing to the condition of her engines, even if the broken shaft could have been repaired.

Leaving the *Maori* behind at Valparaiso, the *Orlando* steamed round the Horn, and after a long and pleasant voyage dropped anchor in Plymouth Sound. Her scientific trophies and the two castaways were all safe. The vessel she had picked up at sea proved a windfall for the Crown.

The story of the castaways proved a windfall for the papers.

Chapter XV.
GOOD-BYE, MARGERY BUTE.

A TELEGRAM from Miss Huntley, Margery's aunt, awaited her in Plymouth. It was delivered on board the cruiser. This message contained an urgent appeal to the girl not to lose a single train to town after she came ashore. The aunt was in poor health or she would have met her niece in person, for the probable date of the cruiser's arrival had been cabled from many points, and there would have been little difficulty on that head. But as Miss Huntley could not come herself she sent a telegram, which must have cost five shillings, and her "companion," Miss Potter, to whose care, under Providence, she committed her niece.

Margery read most of the telegram to Drury. He listened to it with noticeable solicitude. The coolness which had existed between them on the greater part of the voyage home (created, of course, by Margery's regrettable conduct) was forgotten now that the journey was over, and the parting of their ways had come. Margery read the telegram through until she came to the last clause, which, indeed, was a command. She stopped abruptly and in some confusion.

"Why don't you finish it?" Drury asked, carelessly. He had noticed the awkward pause, but did not wish to accentuate the girl's embarrassment. So he made believe to be quite indifferent. Margery laughed and reddened, and made an excuse so very lamely and kept back something from him that was in the telegram so very plainly, he became interested in spite of his effort to appear unconcerned. They were just going on shore: their luggage was over the side; a small knot of officers which had gathered at the gangway suggested the possibility of further farewells—Miss Bute`s farewells. The busy bluejackets passing to and fro on duty glanced toward the lady with respectful regret. The scientific people were gone.

"She describes Miss Potter so well," Margery said, thoughtfully; "that I believe I could easily miss her."

"But you must not do that," Drury exclaimed. "It would cause Miss Huntley great uneasiness, and from what you have told me about her affection for you, she must have suffered very much already. It would not be kind to her."

"It would be disgracefully unkind," Margery agreed. Her emphasis changed his point of view slightly.

"Of course your aunt would know that—that even if you missed the lady I am with you."

"That's where the trouble is. She knows that."

Margery referred again to her telegram, and resumed innocently: "That's why I must find Miss Potter."

"Yes, it is only right. You must find Miss Potter." He spoke cheerlessly.

"And I am to—I am to—lose you. That is my last and most positive instruction. That is the part of the telegram I did not like to read to you."

Drury looked surprised for a moment. Then he said, quietly—"It is best so, Marge—Miss Bute. We are back in civilisation now, and must comply with its formulae. Yes; I will say good-bye here."

"You may if you wish, but I won't," Margery replied with spirit.

"I—er—think you ought to consult your aunt's wishes."

"Oh, there's more than my aunt's wishes to be consulted," she interrupted.

He thought she referred to another relative, and asked—"Who is there, then?"

"There's me," said Margery with more determination than grammar. That disposed of the subject.

Miss Bute graciously said good-bye to the officers once more, and presently the two travellers set foot again on English soil. It was not in one way a cheerful home-coming, for there was not a single soul to welcome them. Miss Potter was waiting comfortably in her hotel, and there was no one else, except the newspaper men, whose enthusiasm could hardly be regarded as disinterested. But after the dangers they had passed, any home-coming was better than none.

Before they called on Miss Huntley's representative they went for a ramble over the town, and afterwards along the wide walks of the Hoe. They found so much of historical interest in Plymouth, to which, of course, they were not giving a thought, that some time slipped by before they remembered duty—and Miss Potter. And even then they surely could not go until they had inspected the monument of Smeaton's genius, Drake's statue, the Armada memorial, and much more. For this elderly lady at whose hotel they were due would entrain them forthwith and carry them off to London town—and to a separation immediate and final. Therefore they were, partly unconsciously, postponing this harsh measure as long as possible.

As to the separation, there need be no doubt about it, for Miss Huntley was a lady of high degree and an immense amount of money, and that George Drury was unlikely to knock at a hall door which might chance to be shut in his face no one knew better than Margery Bute. So they wandered about amongst the mementoes of the past, thinking the while very keenly of the present.

Margery's mood changed. She had been rather silent and depressed; but, with a suddenness that was startling, she became almost boisterous, and seemed to take a delight in teasing Drury by proposing audacious escapades, which he knew would get her talked about, and which in consequence he disputed earnestly. That ought to have weighed with her, especially as she had not the slightest intention of making good any of the bids for notoriety which she described with well-affected glee.

"The sight of a policeman is so reassuring, when one has spent weeks waiting for the war-whoop of a tattooed savage," she explained; "I have not felt so elated since my first holiday from that horrible Belgium school." Her schoolfellows on that occasion had unanimously testified to her excellent spirits. The explanation was more specious than convincing. Drury accepted it with pretended approval.

The call of duty being now sufficiently overdue they made their way, without, however, vulgar haste, to Miss Potter's hotel. Drury did not remain to be introduced. He promised to meet them at a train starting within a couple of hours, raised his hat, said—"Good-bye for the present, Miss Bute," and left her in the hall.

The formal salute was different from the unconventional code into which they had drifted on the Uncharted Island. There, when they met after perhaps a whole day's absence of one or other from the ship, it was just, "Hallo!" answered by "Hallo!" Outwardly as curt and not much more cordial than the frigid etiquette of the public school boy. Yet Margery found herself wondering if the more elaborate greeting was an improvement, as she watched Drury walk away. When he had turned down a cross street she braced herself up to meet Miss Potter, and make the best case she could for herself, versus conventional respectability. And now it became evident that her boisterous good humour was only "nerves," and it was with something very like a little whimper that she entered Miss Potter's room.

Miss Potter was a quiet, kindly little woman whose current object in life was to give thanks for, and to, Miss Huntley. She listened with a gentle expression to the short defence which was set forth, and this soon put the defendant at ease. She said, sympathetically, when the case was closed:

"I am so sorry for you, dear. It is all so very dreadful."

"Oh, it was not all so bad," Margery hastened to correct, fearing that she had been perhaps over boastful of her own courage. "Some of it was pleasant enough."

"It was all absolutely dreadful," Miss Potter interposed, firmly. "Dreadfully improper!"

Margery's defence was shattered by a word, and she stood shamefaced and miserable before the court.

"But, of course, it was not your fault, dearie," the court added, soothingly, as it caressed the culprit; "you could not help that horrid fellow's coming back to the ship after the others had left."

"Thank God he came back," Margery said, fervently.

"Nor prevent his officious attentions!"

"Nor even tried to"—this almost stolidly.

"It must have been awful for you, a—a—alone on that horrible ship." Miss Potter shrank at the thought.

"It would have been awfuller without him."

"Oh, child, child, you must not talk in that dreadful, outspoken way. You are not on the Island now, you know." Miss Potter said this in a tone of reproof, but there was a look in her gentle, old eyes which did not maintain the dignity of the reprimand. Later, when Margery had accepted her friendship by crying agreeably in her arms, she said, with ominous brevity:

"I wonder what your aunt will say about it. She has hardly mentioned it to me yet."

"I don't care what she says," Margery murmured, tearfully.

"He is not—not to come to town with us," Miss Potter added, weakly.

"If he does not wish to, we can't compel him; can we?" Margery whispered, as she stroked the grey hair gently. "And if he does wish to, we can't prevent him; can we?" The stroking hand passed caressingly from the grey hair to the withered cheek.

"But your aunt is most anxious about this."

"So am I," Margery coaxed, and then, after a little more pleading, Miss Potter said, firmly enough for a woman in her position—

"Well, well, dearie, it may be a serious matter for me, but I'll risk it."

Drury had a compartment reserved, and their tickets taken for them, an expense which Miss Potter insisted on being allowed to share. He compromised by accepting the price of her own ticket. To Margery he said—"You don't mind owing me for yours?"

"No," she answered in a whisper; "it is not a large addition to my debt."

As the train swept along through the pleasant English fields, silence fell upon the three persons in the reserved compartment. Two of them found that they had so much to say in the short time now left that it was useless to attempt to say all, so they said nothing. And the lady with the grey hair and the kindly, old face, after several attempts to break the mute monotony, gave up the attempt and went comfortably to sleep—or appeared to do so. Whenever the train stopped, Drury hurried to the refreshment rooms, and returned with edibles of various kinds, which Margery accepted on the condition that she was not expected to eat all right away—that she might spread the feast over the whole of the journey. She knew very well that it was exquisite to him to render these services, and had not, therefore, the heart to deny him. Her splendid spirit of independence had vanished. She was constantly asking him to do silly, little trivialities—buckle a strap round her rugs, fasten her umbrella, which she found it quite impossible to roll, and so on. It was apparent that she would be quite helpless now without him.

It was not, therefore, altogether a surprise to Drury when he had seen the ladies across London and into their suburban train that Margery should give him a card (thoughtfully provided by Miss Potter) with her aunt's address. He thanked her, and said:

"I thought this was to be the end. It is very good of you to give me your address. Mine, for a few weeks, will be—oh, anywhere! Say, the Langham!"

The passengers were all in the carriages, and the train was about to start. The guard was putting his whistle to his lips to give the signal. He was already a minute late. He swung his lamp and blew his blast.

"If you say the Langham, be sure it is the Langham, and—gracious! this dear, old woman is asleep again."

"You should not have stepped on that footboard, sir, when the train was in motion," a porter said, sharply. Drury gave the man half-a-crown to make him hold his tongue. The man thanked him, and walked away, muttering apologetically—

"Very nearly an accident."

George Drury stood on the platform, and, with an abstracted air, watched the train steam out into the darkness. When it had disappeared, he turned and walked slowly up the platform. He looked back once in the direction the train had gone, and said in a low voice:

"Good-bye, Margery Bute."

Chapter XVI.
"NO CARDS."

THE Oceana Shipping Company and the Government corresponded for more than the usual time, and after the orthodox official delay came to an agreement in the form of a compromise over the salvage of the *Maori*. Most of the circumstances of this case were unusual and many absolutely without precedent. Regulations and even Acts of Parliament had to be slightly slurred over. Between the two parties they arranged matters so that George Drury found himself more in pocket than the trifle with which he had started; more indeed than he had ever been before—and more than he ever hoped to be when he was out of heart with fortune and consequently in a pessimistic frame of mind.

The "little cheque" was indeed a windfall as well as a most welcome surprise. He would have been a very rich man with it in his own estimation, but for a paragraph which caught his eye one morning in a weekly paper, devoted to social gossip. This informed him that Miss Margery Bute (only daughter of the late Sir William Bute, whose romantic story of shipwreck and rescue had recently created such a stir, etc. . . . .) had been left the entire fortune of her aunt, Miss Huntley, the well known philanthropist and president of the Society for the Prevention of Wearing High Hats at Theatrical Matinees. Miss Bute, it was said, would reside for the present in the town house of the late Miss Huntley—and so on.

Drury's sense of affluence melted away as he read the paragraph. Rather wealthy at the beginning of it, he was only in comfortable circumstances by the time he was half-way through. When it was finished he belonged to the submerged tenth. "Then there's nothing else for it," he reflected; "but to have another try abroad. I am nearly sure to have better weather this voyage—and certain to have no Margery Bute aboard; which is a pity. Well, well, it can't be helped. What was the good of her getting my address when she has never written. I never could quite make her out. Suppose she has forgotten myself as well as my address." If any other person had supposed, in his presence, that Margery could be so utterly callous, that person would have been sorry presently.

Next minute a letter was handed to him. It was addressed in Margery Bute's writing. He did not open it at once. Opened, it would most likely prove a mere note on some ordinary topic written in the terms of ordinary politeness. Unopened, it served as a stimulant for pleasant thoughts; a firm foundation for a splendid castle—in Spain. Opened, it contained an intimation which could hardly be read otherwise than as a command. With reference to an invitation for the following day it concluded with these words:

"I shall not be 'at home' to-morrow to anyone but you, and I shall wait in all day until you come. So please don't keep me here confined to barracks longer than you can help."

"If she were only a poor girl," Drury reflected as he set out; "it would be so different. Anyhow I must see her before I leave this country for good. And I may as well see her now."

It was unfortunate that as he approached the town house of the late Miss Huntley he met two of the officers of H.M.S. *Orlando*, who were evidently coming from it. They saluted him cheerily and he returned their greeting in the same spirit. He did not wish them to notice his disappointment, and they didn't.

The next meeting was rather embarrassing. The city clothes which Drury felt obliged to wear, and to which he had now for some time been unaccustomed, made him physically as well as mentally uncomfortable. Margery certainly appeared very much at ease in a handsome dress which did her justice. But her conversation was not particularly fluent or *apropos*. It was impossible, of course, for them to fall back on the weather and the new books and such sources of gossip mercifully provided for a reticent race. And somehow they found it impossible to return to the Uncharted Island as a theme for discussion. Miss Potter was out (by special request). Margery spoke out at last:

"I hear you are going abroad somewhere. You are not afraid to try another voyage?"

"To be candid," Drury answered; "I don't quite like the idea of another voyage. But there's really nothing for me to do at home. I have no near relations and not many intimate friends."

"Suppose I don't count?"

Margery's well-marked eyebrows went up and she put on a face of serio-comic dissent. Her big blue eyes were hard to meet.

"I hope I may always count on you as my friend," Drury said gravely, and went on without further reference to the interruption. "There is really nothing for me to do in this country. I should only loaf about. It is too conventional for me."

"I remember that you objected once to a very unconventional life."

"Yes, perhaps I did. But at any rate this country doesn't want me. I must find one which does."

"Which reminds me of something," Margery began in a very hesitating voice; "which I hope you will help me to say. At least, don't make it harder than is necessary. I have a great deal of money now—"

"I am very glad to hear it." He did not look it.

"And I owe you rather a large sum. That is, I owe you my life, consequently I owe you the fortune my aunt left me. But you'll let me off a little easier than that, won't you? Say half!"

"Do you really mean that you are offering me money!" He arose from his chair without knowing what he was doing.

"And if I am offering you money," Margery said warmly; "where's the harm? You saved my life. But for you I should have awoke alone on that island, and remained on it till I died. I can't save your life in return, seeing it is in no danger, and I couldn't help you if it was. Is there anything disgraceful to you or to me in that I wish to help you in the only way in my power. I think you are very unkind and quite superfluously proud to stand on nice points of etiquette—conventional etiquette," Margery added. The thrust was well considered, but it was the tears in her eyes which moved him.

"I don't wish to urge any punctilious argument. But surely you know it was not for money I did—well, what I did—and I don't think I could agree to take money for it. Besides, although it is probably only a stupid tradition, founded on the economic slavery of women in the past—I beg your pardon."— He laughed frankly and went on: "What I meant to say was that the average man simply can't take money from a woman, not even for saving her life, as you say I did yours."

"I don't think the average man is so very particular. You are different," Margery said drily.

She drummed with her foot on the carpet for a minute. It was evident that she need not try to argue with a man who was really a first-rate debater so, as she could not out-argue him, she gave up the attempt. Going to the piano she sat down and played a few bars. Drury started, but did not speak lest she might stop. The murmur of the waves seemed blended with the cords. He had only to close his eyes and the whole scene came back—the slow heave of the long lagoon; the splash of the girl's white fingers in the flashing water; the whistle of the seabirds' wings; the stars of the purple night—

"Oh Genevieve I'd give the world
To live again the lovely past"

Margery stopped singing, and asked in the most casual way:

"Do you remember when and where I last sung that?"

"I shall never forget it," he answered, but did not continue the subject. Margery waited for a moment, and as he remained silent she closed the piano with a snap, and said:

"Well, if you won't let me help you, I can't compel you, and if you must go abroad I suppose you must. I wish you didn't, however. It would be so much pleasanter—for me."

"I really don't see how it could make any difference. I should never come here."

"Oh, shouldn't you?"

"No, I shouldn't. I saw two of the sailor men as I was coming in." He had kept his countenance with the 'sailor men,' as he called them. He did not keep it so well now. The jealous flash in his eyes and the jealous ring in his voice were very apparent—delightfully apparent. Happily, he had not sloughed off all his old barbaric egoism.

"They are really such nice fellows," Margery said, innocently.

"They are perfect gentlemen," Drury agreed. He would not commit himself twice to the same blunder. He could not always control his emotions by his judgment, but he succeeded this time. He hoped that Margery would notice it in his favour. She certainly did notice it to his disadvantage.

There was an awkward pause before she said—

"I didn't see them. I told you I wouldn't be at home to anyone but you. I hope you don't think me too outspoken. It is not as if we were still on the Uncharted Island."

"You certainly were not very outspoken there," Drury admitted.

"It was not easy to be so. I mean that it was not easy to be what I should have wished—*and chaperon myself.*"

It was pretty straight; but he missed it. He thought because the girl had money and he had none, or very little, that it was his duty to get out of the way. He hoped that when he was across the seas she would sometimes give him a kind thought and thank him—thank him most of all for the sacrifice he was making in not taking advantage of her almost open admission that mere gratitude would compel her to say —"Yes." So he hardened his heart.

Margery arose with a petulant gesture, and held out her hand, saying:

"Good-bye!"

"Good-bye!" Drury repeated mechanically. The words were harder to say than he had thought, and he had made a liberal allowance for the difficulty.

"Of course, when you have finally decided upon going, there is nothing more to be said."

"No; I suppose that must be the last word."

He stood fumbling with his hat. The evening sun poured a soft light into the room, and threw long shadows behind the chairs. Everything looked queer. The footsteps in the street sounded strangely. A little way from the house some boys were shouting merrily in a game. A heavily-loaded wagon passed. How very commonplace and yet how curious! He hardly knew why he was waiting. His resolution was sorely tried, but he would not give way. After all, he really was a bit of a hero, though he did not know it and would have denied it.

"You have my best wishes," Margery added rather lugubriously, by way of another last word. She felt the strain of the situation keenly, and knew that, as he was going, it were better he should go quickly. Otherwise she must break down or actually ask him to stay, and she could not bring herself to do that. Of course she knew that he did not wish to go. But he would not give her the least help—and really it was a dilemma. She was equal to it.

"When you are gone," Margery began again shyly, "I shall — shall — miss you very much."

"You will have plenty of society."

"What do I want with society? That wretched island is in every paper. I can't go out without being pointed at and whispered at and giggled at. It does not matter, of course, to you — a man; but it is different with me." She stopped for a moment, and then added in her charmingly demure way—"I am so dreadfully compromised."

. . . .

It was a very quiet affair. "No cards."

PUBLISHER'S ACKNOWLEDGEMENTS
and a note on this edition

ROBERT CROMIE's *The Lost Liner* was originally published in 1898 by R. Aickin & Co. Ltd in Belfast, and Geo. Newes, Ltd in London after which it slipped out of print. This edition marks the first time this book has been made available anywhere since the end of the 19th century.

In making the book available for a new audience we have worked from a first edition copy of the text, making only minor modifications where typographical errors appear to have slipped in during the original typesetting. We have reset the type, and repaginated, otherwise the text is as the original edition, including the use of archaic spellings and punctuation. Here at Avalard we are delighted to be bringing *The Lost Liner* to a new audience.

Cromie's premature death at the age of 51 in April 1907 undoubtedly contributed to the loss of *The Lost Liner* in the popular consciousness, preventing it from being rediscovered following the *Titanic* disaster just five years later in April 1912. Perhaps now a modern audience will be able to appreciate the uncanny connections between the novel and the real life events.

I would like to take this opportunity to thank Diarmuid Kennedy for first introducing me to the writings of Robert Cromie several years ago, and more specifically - to this forgotten gem. My thanks also for his splendid introduction which I hope whets the appetite not only for this tale, but Cromie's work in general, which we hope to be visiting in the near future.

I cannot think of a more appropriate book to launch our range of antiquarian reprints – Avalard Publishing was conceived while I lived in the shadows of Harland and Wolff in East Belfast, and worked just a few hundred yards from Cromie's Ormeau home. As we go to press, in this centenary year of the *Titanic* disaster, Avalard is based in a townland a short distance from Cromie's birthplace in Clough. We couldn't have planned it better if we'd tried.

Robert J.E. Simpson
Annadorn, March 2012

ALSO AVAILABLE FROM AVALARD PUBLISHING

ANNUL DOMINI: THE JESUS FACTOR
by Ingrid Pitt

Time-traveller Robin Firth is dispatched to Galilee via a thought bubble on a mission, but all does not go according to plan. He wakes from his mental journey to find himself trapped in the body of the local madman, Haddaq, with only one thing on his mind – he must reach Jesus and save him from crucifixion...

ANNUL DOMINI is the first in a series of previously unpublished books by the late author and actress Ingrid Pitt. An exciting science-fiction laced alternative look at the familiar passion stories. A thought provoking novel.

Hardback ISBN: 9781908566164
eBook ISBN: 9781908566188

www.avalardpublishing.com
www.ingridpitt.net

ALSO AVAILABLE FROM AVALARD PUBLISHING

ALONG THE SHINING BANN:
MEMOIRS OF AN ULSTER MANOR
by R.M. Sibbett

R.M. Sibbett's ON THE SHINING BANN: RECORDS OF AN ULSTER MANOR was first published in 1928 and is an essential purchase for anyone interested in the history of Mid-Antrim. Sibbett's detailed account of the Manor of Cashel is based on historical records, drawing heavily on a Grand Jury Book (1769-1828) and interviews and provides much information about the local families of Portglenone and environs.

ON THE SHINING BANN is a rich source for those pursuing genealogical research or history relating to the area around Ballymena, Portglenone, Cullybackey, Ahoghill and further afield.

Long out of print, AVALARD PUBLISHING are pleased to be bringing this essential text back into circulation in this facsimile edition via their GORTAHERON BOOKS label. This hardback contains the complete unedited original text of the 1928 edition.

ISBN: 978-1908566249
www.avalardpublishing.com

COMING SOON FROM AVALARD PUBLISHING

STAND AND DELIVER:
TALES OF ULSTER HIGHWAYMEN
by Jim McCallen

Jim McCallen's important text was the first modern appraisal of Irish highwaymen when it appeared in 1993. Detailing the lives and activities of some of the most feared and notorious men in Ulster's history, *Stand and Deliver* is being revised and reissued in 2012 by Avalard Publishing in a new illustrated form.

For more information on this and our other titles visit
www.avalardpublishing.com

Lightning Source UK Ltd.
Milton Keynes UK
UKOW050615310512